2928

Dennis and Maggie—the self-consciously shy hero and heroine of Paul Zindel's uncompromising and moving book

MY DARLING, MY HAMBURGER

Maggie on Dennis. First Date: "How skinny! A face like an undernourished zucchini . . . and always wearing the same baggy sweater."

Dennis on Maggie. First Date: "Her ears were strangely small . . . Her eyes weren't too bad. Maybe they were even a little pretty, but . . . the cockeyed way she'd plucked her eyebrows!"

Paul Zindel is the author of two widely-acclaimed plays:

And Miss Reardon Drinks A Little and
The Effect of Gamma Rays on Man-in-the-Moon Mari-golds, winner of the Pulitzer Prize for Drama.

ABOUT THE AUTHOR

PAUL ZINDEL was born on Staten Island. He has lived in various parts of New York State and in Houston, Texas, where he was Playwright-in-Residence at Nina Vance's Alley Theater under a Ford Foundation Grant.

Mr. Zindel is the author of *The Pigman,* which is being made into a motion picture and which was selected by THE NEW YORK TIMES BOOK REVIEW as one of 1968's Outstanding Books for teen-agers. His plays have been performed at theaters throughout the country, and *The Effect of Gamma Rays on Man-in-the-Moon Marigolds* won the Pulitzer Prize for Drama in 1971.

My Darling, My Hamburger

a novel by Paul Zindel

BANTAM BOOKS
TORONTO · NEW YORK · LONDON

*This low-priced Bantam Book
has been completely reset in a type face
designed for easy reading, and was printed
from new plates. It contains the complete
text of the original hard-cover edition.*
NOT ONE WORD HAS BEEN OMITTED.

🦅

RL 6, IL 10-up

MY DARLING, MY HAMBURGER
*A Bantam Book / published by arrangement with
Harper & Row, Publishers*

PRINTING HISTORY
Harper & Row edition published 1969
*Bantam edition / August 1971
24 printings through December 1978*
25th printing

ISBN 0-553-12741-1

Published simultaneously in the United States and Canada

---

*Bantam Books are published by Bantam Books, Inc. Its trade-
mark, consisting of the words "Bantam Books" and the por-
trayal of a bantam, is Registered in U.S. Patent and Trademark
Office and in other countries. Marca Registrada. Bantam
Books, Inc., 666 Fifth Avenue, New York, New York 10019.*

PRINTED IN THE UNITED STATES OF AMERICA

To My Darling,
My Charlotte Zolotow

part one/the darling

"This is not Ghana."

1

"IT WAS MARIE KAZINSKI who asked how to stop a boy if he wants to go all the way," Maggie whispered.

Liz dragged her trig book along the wall tiles so it clicked at every crack.

"I'll bet she didn't ask it like that," Liz said.

" 'Sexually stimulated' was how she said it, if you must know the sordid details."

"Go on."

"She simply raised her hand," Maggie said, "and asked Miss Fanuzzi in front of the whole class."

"What'd she say?"

"Who?"

"Miss Fanuzzi."

Maggie shifted her books from one arm to the other. "Oh, something dumb. Miss Fanuzzi knows a lot about puberty and mitosis, but I think she needs a little more experience with men."

They moved down the center aisle of the auditorium. Maggie watched Liz scan the crowd. How she envied the way Liz was so conscious of everything that was going on! She could walk into a party and instantly know who was doing what to whom and what they were wearing. Maggie had to look at one thing at a time, and it was always something minuscule, like fingers. She always looked at people's fingers.

"Come to order. I want it quiet in the auditorium!" Mr. Zamborsky, the grade advisor, called out as Maggie took a seat. She jumped when he blew his loud, shrill whistle, *Wrrrrrrrrr!* Liz calmly unwrapped a piece of bubble gum and stuffed it in her mouth. She was still looking over the gathering of seniors that continued to churn and buzz while she lowered herself into the seat next to Maggie.

Wrrrrrrrrr! "We have many important decisions to make at this meeting: Senior Day, the prom, and graduation in June," Mr. Zamborsky started.

"Yahooooooooool" everyone yelled.

"Quiet! I want it quiet!" Mr. Zamborsky screamed.

Liz passed the bubble-gum wrapper to Maggie and watched her read the joke on it: *"At school she was voted the girl with whom you are most likely to succeed."*

Mr. Zamborsky fumbled with a batch of papers, then cleared his throat. "Now I'll turn the meeting over to the class president, Pierre Jefferson."

A young man walked up to the podium. He straightened his tie and smoothed down his hair. "God, Pierre loves himself," Maggie whispered. Liz had slumped down in her seat to read an astrology magazine.

"A big brownie," Liz said.

"I think he's cute," Maggie said.

"The first item on the agenda," Pierre started, "is whether we want the prom formal or semi-formal."

Maggie suddenly felt depressed. She knew it wouldn't matter if everyone were going nude to the senior prom because nobody was going to ask her.

"You think my hair looks OK today?" Maggie asked.

"It looks like thin fungus."

"At least my eyebrows are better, aren't they?"

Liz sat up and turned Maggie's face toward her. "They're cockeyed." She slumped back down.

Maggie sat quietly for a minute. "You're always telling me I need more confidence, and then you tell me I've got cockeyed eyebrows."

"They *are* cockeyed."

Maggie took a hand mirror out of her pocketbook. Liz was right. Everything Maggie did to make herself look better never worked. "Oh, Liz," she wailed, "why didn't you tell me my hair was so messed?"

"I told you it looked like fungus."

"It didn't look bad before I was a wheelbarrow."

"A what?"

"A wheelbarrow. In gym." Maggie stared at herself in the mirror. "Don't you do wheelbarrows?"

"No."

"We've got that new instructor—the sadistic-looking one. Every day she's got half of us lying on the floor, and a squad-mate picks up our legs. We have to walk around on our hands."

Liz yawned and closed the astrology magazine. "She sounds demented." She leaned on the back of the seat in front of her and surveyed the auditorium again.

"Is Sean here?" Maggie asked.

"Front row."

"Where?"

"*There!*"

The class president's voice intruded. "The principal suggested we spend Senior Day at Bear Mountain, as opposed to the customary practice of taking over the school for the day. There were complaints about beer drinking and ungentlemanly behavior . . ."

"What a schnook," Liz sighed.

"Who is that sitting next to Sean? He's with him a lot lately." Maggie sat forward.

"Dennis Holowitz."

"Oh."

Liz smiled strangely. "Sean and I decided we're going to get him to ask you out."

"Oh, Liz, I thought you were my friend! I wouldn't go anywhere with him. He looks weird." He actually was weird-looking, Maggie thought, studying him closely. How skinny! A face like an undernourished zucchini. She chuckled to herself. And always wearing the same baggy green sweater. He must love that sweater. Any time she ever passed him in the halls, there it was, baggy as ever. He wouldn't ask her out anyway.

Liz lowered herself again. She opened her loose-leaf notebook and started reading a love comic hidden inside.

"Miss Fanuzzi said we're going to discuss masturbation tomorrow." Maggie put the mirror back in her pocketbook.

"That's nice." Liz waited a moment, then asked, "What advice did she give for stopping a guy on the make?"

"Who?"

"Miss Fanuzzi," Liz snapped.

"You mean about what to do when things get out of control?" Maggie could tell when Liz Carstensen really wanted to know something because she would start tapping her fingers.

"Yes, stupid."

"Well"—Maggie lowered her voice—"Miss Fanuzzi's advice was that you're supposed to suggest going to get a hamburger."

2

DENNIS HOLOWITZ TRIPPED as he walked up the steps. He hated himself because once again he had been talked into doing something he didn't want to do. When he rang the bell, a troll-like little girl opened the door and started to laugh at him.

"Is Maggie home?"

"Maggie! He's *here!*" The child screamed up the stairs. A stout woman in slacks came to the door.

"Come in, come in," she said. "I'm Maggie's mother." She turned to the little girl. "Did you say hello to the young man, Nora?"

"Hello."

"Nora is Maggie's baby sister."

Dennis tried to smile. "Nice to meet you." He thought Mrs. Tobin was going to explode with joy as she maneuvered him into the house.

"Maggie's father is out on an emergency call, but he'll meet you next time."

"Is he a doctor?" Dennis asked.

"No," Mrs. Tobin replied, "he's a plumber."

Once inside, Dennis almost keeled over from the smell of cooked cabbage. Why was it that any girl he took out had a house with an incredible smell? He had gotten trapped into dating a cousin's boyfriend's sister two months ago, and her house smelled like a mixture of moth balls and Mongolian incense. And his date for the junior prom was a friend of the sister of a girl in his History of America class, and her house smelled

7

like bananas. I'll bet Sean gets Chanel or Shalimar, Dennis thought as he sat down to wait.

"Hello, Dennis," Maggie said as she came down from upstairs.

"Hi."

Maggie looked gigantic in a dark blue dress with a flaring skirt and pinched-in waist, but her hair didn't look too bad—for brown hair.

There was a long silence while everyone waited for his reaction. "You look very pretty tonight," he finally managed. What else could he say?

"Have a nice time," Mrs. Tobin said, opening the front door while she held tightly on to the neck of her youngest child. "What movie are you going to see?"

"*Primitive Love,*" Dennis said.

"Do you think you should?" Mrs. Tobin smoothed the front of her slacks.

"It's a documentary."

"Oh."

As he helped Maggie into the back seat of the car he got a whiff of her perfume. He decided it was Evening in Bayonne.

"Hi." Liz leaned forward so the back of the seat could be pushed forward. Her long blond hair covered the side of her face for a second.

"Hello, Liz." Maggie's dress caught on the door handle. "Hi, Sean," she said, disentangling herself.

Dennis got in the back seat after her, leaving as much room as possible between them. He noticed a little smile on Sean's face as the car started to move.

There was no conversation for the first minute, only the sound of Dennis grinding his teeth. Isn't anyone going to say anything? Maggie wondered.

Liz lit a cigarette. "I saw a girl getting beat up in the parking lot of Richmond Shopping Plaza today."

Maggie was trying to straighten her skirt. "What?"

"Right in broad daylight. They ended up tying her to a telephone pole. I think they were all on pot."

"What are you talking about?"

Maggie leaned forward. For the first time Dennis

noticed her ears were strangely small. At least the right one. He couldn't see the left one at that moment. Her eyes weren't *too* bad. Maybe they were even a little pretty, but he couldn't tell with the cockeyed way she'd plucked her eyebrows.

"The one that started punching her was Gracie Ratinski. I heard she even slaps her own mother around with a dish towel." Liz put the radio on as she spoke.

"She's in my Family Living class," Maggie gasped.

"Who?" Sean asked, trying to concentrate on the driving.

"Gracie Ratinski."

Dennis tried to figure out what it was about Maggie's face that made her unusual tonight. She looked better than when Sean had first pointed her out in the hall. Not exactly a doom date, though categorically she wasn't his type. Probably the worst thing about her was the five-and-ten-cent-store diamond heart she wore on the collar of her dress.

The radio was going a mile a minute and so was Liz. "I heard the girl that got socked was going out with the sailor Gracie brought to the G.O. dance last term."

Sean drove into the parking lot next to the movie house and stopped the car. "We're late," he said, obviously annoyed.

"Do you like my dress?" Maggie asked while the boys were buying the tickets.

"It looks like you made it," Liz said.

"I did."

"It looks it."

"You don't have to keep saying it. I guess the pleated front makes me look fatter—"

"Oh, Maggie, you're supersensitive," Liz said. "Dennis won't be looking at the pleats."

"I feel ill."

"The pleats make you look very feminine."

Maggie looked at Liz closely to see if she was telling the truth. "Are you sure?"

Liz put her cigarette out by grinding it into the lobby rug.

"Do you want popcorn?" Dennis asked.

"Oh, yes," said Maggie without thinking. Then she noticed Liz wasn't getting any, even though she liked popcorn as much as Maggie. It was a mistake.

"This movie's supposed to be fantastic," Dennis said, handing her the bag of popcorn. "They show you pygmies chopping the head off a water buffalo."

Maggie frowned. "That's disgusting."

Sean walked up the balcony steps with Liz. Maggie started up after them while Dennis was getting a drink from an ornate water fountain in the lobby. She looked at Liz's graceful walk and tried to imitate her, but she knew she'd be lucky if she could even get up the stairs without tripping.

Sean led the way into the last row of the balcony. Liz followed, and Maggie pushed past Dennis.

"Are you all right?" Liz asked.

"Yes," Maggie said. "I just wanted to make sure I sat next to you." The picture had already started.

HERE THE WAMBESI TRIBE GET MOST OF THEIR FOOD. A DIET OF COCONUT MILK, GOOCHIE BERRIES, AND INSECT LARVAE ARE ALLEGED TO BE A POTENT APHRODISIAC FOR THE NATIVES. THE "SPIRIT OF THE THOUSAND MOONS" WHO DWELLS IN THIS RAIN FOREST IS WORSHIPED AS A DEITY . . .

"Would you like to take your coat off?" Dennis asked.

"Thank you, no." Maggie moved farther away from him.

"What's an aphrodisiac?" Liz asked loudly.

"A love potion," Dennis said.

How does he know a word like that? Maggie wondered.

She rearranged her left arm because her slip strap was too tight, and her elbow hit his arm. He had completely taken over the armrest. She moved her arm again, but the strap was still uncomfortable.

Plunk. Her pocketbook dropped.

"I'll get it," Dennis said.

A man in the next row turned around. "*Shhhhh.*"

"Shut up, yourself," Liz snapped.

"I've got it," Maggie said, bending over quickly and using the movement to adjust the strap.

THE CHILDREN BORN TO THE WOMEN OF THE WAMBESI ARE RAISED BY THE ENTIRE TRIBE. EVERY MALE MEMBER IS CONSIDERED THE FATHER AND EVERY FEMALE THE MOTHER. THIS LACK OF A FAMILY UNIT AS WE KNOW IT TENDS TO ELIMINATE MANY OF THE ANXIETIES KNOWN TO OUR CULTURE. . . .

Does she think I'm going to put my arm around her? Dennis wondered. She's given me enough hints, tapping my arm. Out of the corner of his eye he could see Sean already making out with Liz.

THE COSTUMES OF THE WAMBESI ARE A DELIGHT TO BEHOLD. THE EQUATORIAL CLIMATE RENDERS THEIR DRESS BRIEF BUT RESPLENDENT WITH THE COLORS OF THE RAIN-BOW. THEY DYE THEIR VEGETABLE FIBERS WITH PIG-MENTS OBTAINED FROM VARIOUS FLOWERS AND BERRIES, AND YOU WILL NOTICE IN THE ATTIRE OF THE WOMEN A VARIETY OF HUES. THE PLUMAGE OF THE EXOTIC TOUCANET IS ESPECIALLY PRIZED. . . .

If he puts his arm around me, I'll tell him to move it, Maggie thought. I'll say it firmly but nicely and try not to hurt his feelings. God, what a loud yellow shirt he's wearing!

Dennis loosened his tie. She's not even watching the movie, he thought. She's sitting there waiting for me to hold her hand or something. She can wait until the year 5000 before that. And if she thinks I'm going to kiss her goodnight, she is delirious.

What if he started pressing against me and

wouldn't stop? Maggie worried. He had several hairs growing on his upper lip, so he could be overly mature for his age. Liz letting Sean kiss her right in the theater wasn't helping either.

Dennis tried to watch the picture. Maybe she expects me to go all the way tonight, he thought. She's quiet, but so was Barbara Johnson, and she entertained eleven seniors in the parking lot behind the Hollywood Diner.

Maggie turned her back slightly while she smoothed down the pleats on the front of her dress. She knew Dennis was watching her, and the way he was squirming was frightening. And all those nude natives running around on the screen was unbelievable. He'd probably never ask her out again. She knew that was what she was really worried about most. The dress hadn't come out right, but she thought the heart-shaped diamond pin made her look a little nice— a little.

Dennis could tell she knew he was watching her out of the corner of his eye, so he made believe he wasn't. Then he started to think about walking her to the door at the end of the evening. He wouldn't get out of the car. Let her go by herself. That way she couldn't corner him into a kiss. One thing was for sure. He wouldn't take her out again. Not in a million years.

THE WAMBESI ARE INDEED A BEAUTIFUL PEOPLE. THEY LIVE WITHOUT SHAME, AND EVEN THE FACES OF THEIR ELDERS SEEM TO REFLECT THE SERENITY AND LOVE WHICH ABOUNDS AMONG THEM. THIS SMILING GROUP WAVES AT THE CAMERA, EXEMPLIFYING THE HAPPINESS OF THEIR LIFE IN THE RAIN FOREST. IF YOU LOOK CLOSELY AT THE SMALL BOY IN THE CENTER, YOU WILL NOTICE HE IS HOLDING A SHRUNKEN HEAD . . .

Liz:

I'm writing this in Miss Blair's class. She's wearing a tight yellow knit suit today, and she looks like a sunburst. I want you to know how much I appreciated your getting me the date last night, but I don't think Dennis liked me too much. He passed me in the hall 2nd period, and he didn't even say <u>hello</u>.

I'll see you outside the cafeteria 5th, but I wanted you to get this before if I can find someone to deliver it to you in Trig.

XXX

Love,

Maggie

P.S. I had a nightmare about the Wambesi.

3

SEAN RARELY THOUGHT OF SUICIDE anymore, although he used to think about it often. He had ruled out an overdose of sleeping pills because he knew all they did was relax the diaphragm, and to him that was the same as suffocating to death. He decided the best way would be a .357 magnum pistol—the kind the police use when they want a bullet to pass through the engine block of a car. If he placed the barrel at his temple, the force would be enough to blast his head off his body. He had done some calculations using the Law of Conservation of Momentum.

$$\begin{array}{ccc}
\text{MASS} \times \text{VELOCITY} & = & \text{MASS} \times \text{VELOCITY} \\
\text{(Head)} \quad \text{(Head)} & & \text{(Bullet)} \quad \text{(Bullet)}
\end{array}$$
$$2{,}000 \text{ grams} \times X = 40 \text{ grams} \times 50{,}000 \text{ cm./sec.}$$

According to his figures, his head would fly off at a velocity of about one thousand centimeters per second.

He had no intention of actually committing suicide, but he used to think about it a lot. Maybe he thought about it a little more than other kids. He just didn't care very much about living.

He had decided once what he hated most about life was the human race. It was pathetic. It depressed him just to ride a bus and look at the people. Tired. Washed out. Useless. A fat woman with a shopping bag, her seams splitting apart while she held a bakery box on her lap. A skinny man pretending to read a newspaper so he wouldn't have to look some standing cripple in the eye and offer him his seat. A woman with perspiration stains on her dress. Another man eating pretzels and looking like he hadn't taken a bath in a year. What the hell was there to live for? To turn into monstrosities like those? Life was one huge pathetic waste as far as he was concerned.

Until Liz.

He had first noticed her in the halls at school a year ago. She had been around before that, but she used to have her hair cut short, and she kept very much to herself. It was just after summer vacation when she showed up in his chemistry class. A few of the boys had pushed to date her, but they had no luck. Then he had asked her out, and she turned him down. "I'm sorry," she had said, as though she were refusing to donate to some charity.

He had told her off. "*Who the hell do you think you are?*" He remembered how shocked she looked when he said that. Before he fell asleep that night he could still see her. Her voice had sounded so snobbish, but her eyes haunted him like those of a wounded fawn. The thought crossed his mind that maybe she was as depressed and disgusted with living on this planet as he was—that the tone of her voice was a defense, like the endless defenses he had erected between himself and the world. And that was the moment he decided to handle her as if she was a frightened animal.

The next day he asked her out again and she refused. This time he was the one who said "I'm sorry." And the next day he asked her again. Every day for two weeks he asked her out. He checked the attendance book in her register class for her telephone number, and on weekends he called her house. Finally she started to smile when he passed her in the halls. Then one day she said Yes.

"What?" he asked.

"Yes," she repeated.

They had gone to a picnic on the first date, but all

they did was talk—and laugh. He remembered feeling like a creature from outer space who after a million years of banishment from his home planet had at last found another exile. Two foreign spirits trapped under human skins were finally able to breathe.

He had reminded Dennis of these first experiences with Liz in order to get him to take Maggie out a second time.

"I wouldn't mind," Dennis had said, "if Maggie's foreign spirit were hidden under an exterior like Liz's."

Sean laughed.

"It's not funny," Dennis protested.

"Would you rather stay home all your life?"

"No."

"It's good experience."

"It's an experience all right."

On the night of their second double-date Sean left the car running while he went into a delicatessen. None of them drank much, but a beer tasted good while walking along the beach.

The old man behind the counter was scratching his face. "What do you want?"

"A six-pack of H & R."

Sean looked around while the old man hobbled to a huge refrigerator and fumbled through the many cans.

"Make sure they're cold."

"They're *all* cold," the man grunted.

A three-foot replica of the Empire State Building made out of toothpicks was standing on top of the meat freezer. It was faded and looked ready to topple. Sean moved closer to read the newspaper clipping attached to the bottom of it. Its date was almost thirty years old, and there was a picture of the owner with his toothpick Empire State Building. He was looking directly into the camera. It was sad to think of anyone sitting down and gluing all those toothpicks together. How useless.

When Sean got back to the car, he had to laugh at

the way Maggie and Dennis were sitting so far apart
in the back seat.

"You don't want a beer?" Liz asked.

Maggie's voice broke slightly. "No, thank you."

"We're off," Sean said, stepping on the accelerator.

The road to Marine Park Beach had no streetlights,
and Sean had to drive carefully to avoid hitting the
scores of rabbits darting out of the bulrushes. Some
stared from the sides of the road, their eyes glowing
in the headlights. They looked like little glaring
ghosts.

"Slower," Liz pleaded. "You'll run over them."

He stopped the car next to one of them. It was
sitting up staring, frozen.

"Hi, bunny!" Liz hung out the window.

The animal ran away, its tiny white tail bouncing
up and down like a Ping-Pong ball.

"He was so scared," Maggie said.

Liz was already walking along the beach by the
time Sean got the blanket out of the trunk. He smiled
at Dennis and left him and Maggie in the back seat.

He caught up with Liz before she reached the
water. She was staring straight at the sky. "What are
you looking for?" he asked.

"Andromeda," she said.

"What?"

"A constellation."

Her voice was too energetic. Too quick. She must
have had another fight at home.

Sean had learned not to ask her about those troubles. Sometimes she'd talk about them of her own
accord. Of course, they had arguments of their own
now and then. They both had tempers. But they were
beginning to know what to push and what to leave
alone.

He spread the blanket and sat down, smoothing the
sand beneath it. Then he stretched out with the can
of beer on his chest and raised his head just enough
to see Liz standing near the edge of the surf. A wave

broke close to her, and she jumped back. She was beautiful even when she was angry over something.

"Come over here," he called.

Still looking at the sky, she moved toward him. When she was close enough, he reached out his hand to pull her down.

"No," she said, settling into a kneeling position. "I think it's over there. Near the moon."

"What?"

"Andromeda."

Then she flopped down and propped her elbows on his stomach. He jumped from her weight, and they laughed.

The words of the new astrology book she had bought kept running through her mind. It was such an unusual one, with predictions that were much more severe than the usual kind. Most of the books read the same whether you were Taurus or Capricorn or Cancer. Only nice things were going to happen. But this one was another story. It had been advertised in the back of a love comic, and she hadn't been able to resist sending for it.

YOU ARE A SELFISH, PASSIONATE INDIVIDUAL WHO HATES WITH THE STRENGTH OF A SCORPION'S POISON AND LOVES WITH THE MADNESS OF A GYPSY. IT IS IN YOUR NATURE TO STEAL, AND UNLESS YOU PRAY TO THE MADONNA YOU WILL BE PUNISHED FOR THIS SIN AS WELL AS YOUR SINS OF OMISSION. YOU EMBRACE LIFE WITH GLUTTONY, AND UN-LESS YOU CONTROL YOUR APPETITE YOU WILL SUFFER MUCH PAIN. ONE DAY YOU COULD MURDER. PRAY TO THE MADONNA. ON SUNDAYS PRAY TO THE MADONNA. PRAY THAT GOD WILL FORGIVE YOUR LUST.

She could see a small rock island about a mile off shore. A light there kept blinking on and off. Perhaps that was where Andromeda had been chained, she thought. It was the only myth she had studied in school that stayed with her—the only one that had meaning for her. Her people were being devoured by a sea serpent as decreed by the gods in punishment for the sins of her country. She could feel the chains around her ankles and see the water ripple away from the surfacing monster. It came toward her, and she wondered if anyone would save her. That was the way she had felt not so long ago. In the myth it was Perseus who saved Andromeda. For her it had been Sean.

"I need you," Sean whispered.

She loved being near him. He made her feel secure and happy. When he touched her hand or pressed against her, she was certain there was a special chemistry between them. If only he could be satisfied with what they had been doing—at least for now.

He was kissing her deeply. This feeling was something she never felt with any other boy, and she was frightened at how naturally she had learned to enjoy their closeness.

"*Please*," he said softly. He made her look at him. "We love each other, don't we?"

She couldn't answer.

"Please ..."

"No."

His voice became suddenly angry. "Why not?"

The first time they had reached this point, she had felt hurt when his voice changed like that. Now she was hardened to it.

He waited a moment, and she could see he was trying to control his temper.

"No!" She got up from the blanket.

"Then take pills or something!"

He got up but wouldn't look at her. Then he started to fold up the blanket. He knew it was wrong, but he couldn't stop himself from saying it.

"You're a pain in the ass, you know that?"

"You like swimming?" Maggie asked.

"It's all right," Dennis replied. "Do you like it?"

"It's nice in the summer."

"It's too cold now."

"Yeah."

"Where do you go swimming when it's warm enough?" Maggie pursued.

"Down here—or else Wolf's Pond. Lot of rocks there."

"I heard that."

"It's true."

Maggie noticed his left hand getting closer every minute, and his fingers were tapping like a pneumatic drill. She felt as though it were a spider getting ready to drop on her shoulder.

"I was here the day Mel Haughting drowned."

"Really?" Maggie was interested. Mel Haughting had been in her chemistry class.

"They were stoned and were out on a raft over *that* way." Dennis pointed. "He got stuck under it, and nobody noticed until it was too late."

She looked impressed, he thought. Maybe he ought to try kissing her. Make his move just for the heck of it. Chalk it up to experience. Liz and Sean wouldn't be back for a little while, and even if she slapped him, it wouldn't matter.

He moved closer. She pretended to be looking in the other direction. He turned her head toward him. His lips touched hers. Almost. The kiss was on the left side of her mouth, but with a little wiggle everything lined up all right.

He kept his lips pressed against hers for a few moments, and he was surprised she didn't pull away. "*She's letting me kiss her*," he told himself. "*She's letting me kiss her.*" In the middle of the kiss he opened his eyes, and he almost jumped. She was looking right back at him!

"I th ... th ... th ... think" she stuttered. "I think we'd better go get a hamburger."

FROM THE OFFICE OF SENIOR GUIDANCE

TO: Sean Collins   REGISTER   71-8

You have been recommended for English Honors Class
12HX. Report to Room 312 instead of your regular
English, starting Monday 10/18.

                              Mr. Karl Zamborsky
                              Senior Grade Advisor

(P.S. Your essay on suicide was
fascinating!)

4

Mrs. Palladino let the phone ring several times before she answered it on the bedroom extension. Then she pulled her robe tight around herself and went to the top of the stairs.

"It's for you, Liz," she called down.

"Who is it?"

"That Collins boy." Mrs. Palladino went back to her bedroom, leaving the door open.

"Tell him I went out with somebody else!" Liz waited at the bottom of the stairs for her mother's reaction.

"I will not!"

"Then say I came down with a bad case of beri-beri."

Mrs. Palladino picked up the receiver and hesitated before speaking. "I'm sorry, but Liz doesn't want to talk to you, Sean." She hung up and then went to the top of the stairs again.

"I want to talk to you."

"About what?"

"Get up here."

Liz was thankful to hear the shower running behind the closed bathroom door. Her mother was sitting at her dresser, meticulously styling her silver hair. It was much too stiff and unnatural, but she wouldn't listen to anything Liz told her about it.

"You're going out again?" Liz asked.

Mrs. Palladino managed an affirmative nod while

she concentrated on a wave that didn't shape the way she wanted. "We're invited to the Stanleys'. They might sponsor us for the club."

"That's nice."

Mrs. Palladino caught the inflection in her daughter's voice. "Did you notice the Madonna I put on your dresser, dear?"

"Yes," Liz said impatiently.

"Since you refuse to go to church with me . . ." Mrs. Palladino decided to approach the point differently. "I mean, since at this time in your life you don't seem to have much use for religion, I thought you should at least have the Madonna in your room.

Liz looked at her a moment. "You didn't call me up here to talk about heaven."

Her mother paused, then smiled, embarrassed. "Liz, I also wanted to talk to you about that boy."

Liz leaned against the doorway and took a deep breath. "What about him?"

"Is Sean a nice boy?"

"What's a *nice* boy?"

"You know what I mean."

"You met him."

"Don't be fresh, Liz." Mrs. Palladino held a hairpin in her mouth but it didn't stop her from continuing. "Your father doesn't like it when you speak to me like that."

"You mean my *stepfather*."

Liz heard the shower being turned off and wanted to get out of the room before he opened the door.

"You're not doing anything you shouldn't—that's what I mean."

Liz laughed.

Mrs. Palladino wrinkled her brow. "You're being very rude, Elizabeth."

Liz could tell from her mother's glances toward the bathroom door that even she wanted the discussion finished before her husband came out.

"I mean"—Mrs. Palladino paused—"the boy isn't

taking drugs or anything like that? So many of them are, I hear."

"No," Liz smiled. "Sean isn't taking drugs this week. Is your husband?"

"Liz, I try to talk to you the best I know how, but you make it so hard. I don't know what you want from me."

"Not a thing."

"I'm worried about you."

Liz laughed. "Worried?" She pointed to the bathroom door. "Why didn't you worry about me before you married him?"

Mrs. Palladino threw her comb down on the dresser and turned away from the mirror. At that moment the bathroom door opened, and Mr. Palladino came into the room, barefoot and wearing a black silk robe. There was something powerful, almost bearlike about the way he walked. He stopped at the bureau and looked at them for a moment.

"What's the matter now?"

Mrs. Palladino turned back to the mirror. "I was just asking Liz about the boy she's dating. She's been staying out late."

"That's my business," Liz said.

Mr. Palladino opened the top bureau drawer. He started back toward the bathroom with a set of clean underwear over his arm. He stopped at the doorway and turned to Liz. "What you do, young lady," he said slowly and calmly, "is going to get you a good slap across the face one of these days."

"I'm not out late."

"If your mother says it's late, it's late. You'll be in this house by midnight Fridays and Saturdays. Nine o'clock any other night." Mr. Palladino looked at her from deep-set angry eyes. "Do you understand me, Elizabeth?"

When the phone rang, Maggie was afraid it would be Dennis canceling their date.

"Hello?"

"Maggie?"

She breathed a sigh of relief. "Hello, Liz. I was going to call to see what you are wearing."

"I'm not wearing anything. I decided not to go."

"You're not?"

"No," Liz said. "I hate Sean Collins. Call Dennis and tell him you can't make it either."

Maggie gasped. "I can't do that."

"I'll explain later."

"But he's supposed to pick me up in a half hour."

"Tell him you forgot you had to visit a sick aunt in the hospital."

"I can't say that."

"You said he was a goon," Liz reminded her. "Right in the auditorium you said he looked like a goon."

"He'll feel funny."

"Goons are *supposed* to feel funny."

Maggie felt numb as she hung up the phone. Why was everything so complicated? She should have refused to break the date. But she wouldn't have had any date if it wasn't for Liz. Liz had always been a good friend. This must be something important. She'd have to break the date.

"Aren't you dressed yet?" Mrs. Tobin was in the kitchen, cleaning the stove.

Maggie tried to think of the simplest way to explain.

"I have to call Dennis and say I have a headache and can't go."

"Why? You look fine."

"Liz had another fight."

"Oh," Mrs. Tobin said calmly, slipping out each of the black iron burner-tops and soaking them in a pan of ammonia. "With Sean or her family?"

"Both, I think."

"Poor Liz. Is her stepfather really so mean?"

Maggie hesitated before answering. She didn't like to tell too much about Liz to anyone, but sometimes her mother had very good advice. Sometimes. She decided to change the subject.

"Mother?"

"What, Maggie?"

"Do you think Dennis is nice-looking?"

Mrs. Tobin went to the sink and got a piece of steel wool. "He's cute."

"Really?"

"Yes. And he's respectful. That was something I liked about your father when we were first going out. Couldn't stand my parents, and they hated him—but he was respectful. That's very important." She crossed back to the stove.

"You think so?"

"I do." Mrs. Tobin rubbed a stubborn grease spot extra hard. "You did a good job on the dishes tonight," she said.

"Thank you."

"Has he kissed you yet?"

Maggie blushed.

"Good. He's supposed to." Mrs. Tobin smiled. "Do you enjoy being with him?"

"A little."

"That's nice." Mrs. Tobin got down on her hands and knees to check the back of the broiler. "A boy doesn't have to look like a prince to make a good husband. That bald-headed man out there in our living room was never a raving beauty, you know. But he loves me." She looked up at her daughter. She touched her hair, aware of how disheveled she looked. "I love him too."

"Yes, Mother."

"Believe me, Maggie, you've got to love somebody to clean a dirty broiler. You've got to."

"Dad!"

"We're in the den," Mr. Collins called back as he stirred a batch of martinis.

Sean came to the doorway. When he saw that his

father had company, he decided he'd say hello and leave.

"Come on in," Mr. Collins boomed heartily. "You know Mr. Wilson and Mr. Stanley?"

"I don't want to interrupt."

"Hell, no. You come on in here. We're just talking about some of the good old college days—with a little straight business between halves." He slapped Mr. Stanley on the back, and the three laughed heartily.

"Hello," Sean said.

"Looks like you're going to have another football player in the family." Mr. Stanley beamed.

"Long as he applies himself, right, son?" Mr. Collins said. He put his arm around Sean for a moment. Then he refilled the glasses sitting in front of his guests. "Got a sixty-eight in physics, didn't you?"

"Yes, Dad."

"You're not going to play football anywhere with a sixty-eight in physics. Is he, boys?"

"I got a ninety-six in English."

"You're *supposed* to know English. It's physics. Physics. That's where the money is. Anybody'll tell you that. Right, Dan? Or chemistry. Mr. Wilson's in chemistry, you know."

"Dad . . ."

"Something the matter?" Mr. Collins asked.

"No."

"Need a little extra for your date?"

"I'm not seeing Liz tonight."

"What?" Mr. Collins let out one of his raucous laughs. He put his arm around Sean again and practically marched him closer to the smiling faces of Mr. Wilson and Mr. Stanley. "Saturday night and my boy's not going out. What happened with that little blond wildcat?"

"Dad . . ."

"She's giving you a hard time?"

Sean couldn't answer.

Mr. Collins turned to the others. "He's going hot and

heavy with that Carstensen girl. Did you ever see her?"

Sean resented his father's tone and turned to get his arm off his shoulder. "She's a nice girl."

"You can say that again." Mr. Collins sat down, with an insinuating laugh. Mr. Wilson and Mr. Stanley joined in. Sean looked at the three of them sitting in their deep plush chairs, and they reminded him of squatting Buddhas.

Then Mr. Collins spoke seriously. "Then what's the problem?"

Sean looked directly into his father's eyes. He wished that one day he could manage to talk to him—just talk, without all the put-on.

"Nothing," he said.

"Dinner is on the table, Dennis."

"Be right there, Mom."

"Wash your hands."

Dennis looked at himself in the bathroom mirror. He felt sick. Just sick. He could tell from Maggie's voice on the phone she was just making up the excuse to break the date. She sounded so guilty.

"Dennis!"

"I'm coming."

Mr. and Mrs. Holowitz were waiting for him at the table. They were always formal about dinner. The correct fork had to be used. The bread had to be broken before buttering it. Even if it was sausage and sauerkraut, they made a ceremony of it. The dining room was not elegant. No silver candelabra like at Sean's house. No flowers on the table. It was a plain old dining room, with scratched but polished furniture. There was always a tablecloth and cloth napkins —even if they didn't match. His parents meant well, but there was a lot of the old Polish in them.

"Chew your food, Dennis."

"Yes. Mother."

He didn't feel much like eating because his stomach was upset from the phone call. Just when he was beginning to think Maggie liked him! The way she let him kiss her on the last date—once in the car and once at her door. He couldn't understand. Maybe he had halitosis. He had gargled before the date. The bottle said to do it for fifteen seconds. He had done it for over a minute. It felt like half the epithelial cells had been gargled off his tongue.

"Your mother tells me you didn't put the garbage cans out today," Mr. Holowitz said grimly, looking over the silver rims of his glasses. His voice was quiet but stern.

"I forgot."

Perhaps Maggie thought he was too weird-looking. A weird body. He had grown so quickly he was taller than his mother or father. But he was *so* skinny, and his feet and hands had grown so big. He hated taking his socks off at night because his feet looked like they didn't belong to him. A year ago they were small, and now they looked like surfboards.

Mrs. Holowitz wiped her mouth with her napkin. "You should rinse the cans out with the hose. The coffee grounds stick to the bottom."

"Yes, Mom."

Mr. Holowitz hurriedly finished chewing a mouthful of sauerkraut in order to contribute further to the discussion. "Use warm water and disinfectant."

"I'll do that."

"Would you like some more sausage, Dennis?"

"No thanks, Mom."

Dennis looked down at his plate and cut a boiled potato into neat geometric portions. Halves, then quarters, then eighths, then sixteenths.

Maybe his deodorant had failed. He had used the roll-on kind he got for Christmas, *and* his father's spray type—plus spice talcum and aftershave lotion. Not a lot—a little of each everywhere. Everywhere. Oh, God, he was sick. What didn't she like about him?

Mrs. Holowitz had finished eating and sat up straight at the table. Her small delicate hands were neatly placed in her lap. Dennis knew she was looking at him. She never said much, but she seemed to know what he was thinking.

"Was that the young lady on the phone?"

"Yes, Mom." Dennis squirmed on the chair during the silence that followed. He knew they were curious about why any girl would call a boy at his house. They wouldn't understand, and he didn't feel up to telling the truth.

"She said she'd be a half hour late getting ready."

"That was nice of her to call," Mrs. Holowitz said.

There was another silence.

"This girl you're going out with," Mr. Holowitz said, tracking the last strands of sauerkraut with his fork, "you make sure you respect her, young man. Understand me?"

"Yes, Father."

"Respect her."

November 17
The Dumpy Cafeteria

Maggie:
Since lunch I went to gym and cut 7th period. I'm sending this via Helen Mackey if she goes to your 9th. Just had to tell you they started doing wheelbarrows in gym. I refused.!!! I told the looney teachers I was under the care of a chiropractor and he said wheelbarrows weren't good for me.

Have you seen Sean? He hasn't called me all week. I don't care. If you see him, make sure you tell him I don't care.

XXXXX

Ha! → Liz Carstensen

5

Liz, I'm getting tired."

"Shut up and keep walking." Liz was several feet in front of Maggie as they marched along the curbless side of Hyland Boulevard. The car headlights were blinding.

"Is it much farther?" Maggie asked.

"What?"

"The Red Pub Inn."

Liz stopped and lit a cigarette. Maggie caught up to her. "Some guys'll pick us up any minute," Liz said.

"I'm not getting in a strange car."

"You are *so* out of it," Liz mumbled, and she started off again. Maggie made a desperate attempt to keep up with her.

"Are my slacks too tight?" Maggie asked.

"Of course they are," Liz said. "They're supposed to be."

"Why is it," Maggie protested, "tight slacks make you look gorgeous and make me look like a rhinoceros?"

"You look like dynamite," Liz said, scooting ahead.

Maggie skipped a few steps to catch up again. She wished she hadn't broken that date with Dennis. She knew he hadn't believed her. That was why he hadn't called since.

"I'm not getting in a strange car," Maggie repeated.

"Yes, you are."

"No, I'm not."

"Hey, girls! Want a lift?" A boy with glasses leaned out the window of a shiny yellow Pontiac.

"Beat it," Liz said, and she kept walking.

Even after the car had gone, Maggie's heart was pounding. She wasn't used to doing things like walking along a highway at night and lying and having strangers yell things out. In fact, *anything* unusual upset her.

"Did you know the boy in that car?" Maggie asked.

"No."

"It was only *one* boy, wasn't it?"

"Yep." Liz marched on.

Maggie thought a moment, then was curious. "He looked safe, didn't he?"

"Too safe," Liz said. "I don't mind a lift, but I do mind a fruit."

Maggie's feet were beginning to hurt. The buses ran only every hour, and Liz had insisted on walking. They'd covered over two miles already, and she was ready to drop. Every few feet something new began to ache. Now it was her left knee. She could feel the bones clicking. And her right index finger had fallen asleep. The weight of her pocketbook had cut off the circulation in two fingers. One had woken up, but the other was still tingling. That, together with the exhaustion of marching, the headlights blinking, boys yelling things from cars, a clicking knee, and the gnawing thought of Dennis was about all she could bear.

Liz was several yards ahead when an old red Cadillac convertible screeched to a halt. She had already disappeared into the interior by the time Maggie caught up. A tall good-looking boy had gotten out and was smiling at her.

"Get in," he said.

Maggie maneuvered herself reluctantly into the back seat. She felt as if she was climbing into a blue-leather tomb. The smiling boy swung in next to her.

"Maggie," Liz said, tossing the remains of her cigarette into the street and pressing a button so the window closed electrically, "that's Don McHugh back there. This is Rod Gittens."

"Hello, Maggie." Rod twisted his head around to get a better look. Don smoothly put his hand on the seat in back of her.

Suddenly the car burned rubber and shot out into the traffic. The bolt was so unexpected Maggie's head hit Don's arm.

"Where you girls going?" Rod asked in a rich, friendly voice.

"The Red Pub," Liz replied.

Maggie noticed the boy next to her moving closer. She had caught her bracelet on a chrome accessory on the left side of the car.

"Let me get it for you," Don offered politely.

"Thank you," Maggie said. The tone of his voice put her immediately at ease. In fact, both of the boys seemed to be well-groomed and considerate. Besides, Liz knew them.

"Do you miss school?" Liz asked the boy named Rod.

"I have my career now," he said. He drove with one hand on the wheel and the other across the top of the seat. "I'm at Dongan Memorial Hospital."

Liz pressed the button again and opened the window halfway. "No kidding."

"Yes."

"What do you do?"

The boy flipped his head, sending his long sand-colored hair precisely into place.

"Inhalation therapy."

"What's that?" Liz asked.

"Oxygen. I work with oxygen."

Suddenly Maggie felt herself flying through the air as the car braked to a halt. Don caught her before she banged her head on the front seat. She was thankful he had.

Liz opened the door and jumped out. "Come on, Maggie, here's the Red Pub."

"A pleasure meeting you," Don said. He let Maggie out and climbed into the front.

"You girls sure you wouldn't rather take a ride?" Rod asked.

Maggie bit her lip and waited for Liz to answer, for there was something about the way Don had treated her that was both kind and exciting. He was so good-looking. She had never seen him before in her life, but she liked him. He was certainly a hundred times better-looking than Dennis Holowitz, and he seemed to like her.

"No," Liz said. She started away from the car. "Thanks for the lift."

"You sure?" Don called after her.

"Positive!" Liz yelled.

Maggie stood for a moment, looking at the boys. She felt a little embarrassed at the way Liz had been so rude. She tried to think of a polite way to say good-bye but couldn't get the words out. She awkwardly backed away from the car.

"It was really a pleasure meeting you," Don said. His voice was deep and sincere.

"Thank you." Maggie smiled.

"Yes, indeed." Then he added with an innocent smile, "And you've got a nice pair of knockers."

There was a squeal of tires. Maggie stood on the curb. She was dumbfounded—absolutely dumbfounded. Liz had to come back and get her.

"They're just pigs," Liz said, taking her hand and leading her toward the flashing neon sign of the bar. "The one in front, Rod, quit school two years ago after he got a freshman pregnant. Been riding around in that old crappy Caddie ever since."

Maggie sounded like a little girl. "They seemed so nice."

"They'd beat their mothers for beer money," Liz said, looking in a side window of the bar. The reflection from a streetlight forced her to cup her hands over her eyes in order to see inside.

"Is Sean there?" Maggie asked. If he was, maybe Dennis would be with him.

"Nope." Liz pushed her hair out of her eyes and started for the front door. "We'll take one of the back booths."

"Liz, we can't go in *there*. We're not old enough."

"They never ask for proof." Liz kept heading for the entrnce.

"They'll ask me!"

Liz stopped and took an objective look at Maggie. She decided they probably would ask her. Quickly she opened her purse and pressed a frayed piece of paper in her hand.

"What's this?"

"Somebody's birth certificate. Remember, your name is Catherine Usherer tonight," Liz assured.

"I can't do that!"

"Why not?"

Maggie could hardly find her voice. "They'll know I'm lying."

"No, they won't," Liz insisted. "Unless, of course, they've already checked the *real* Catherine Usherer's ID."

"How did you get Catherine Usherer's birth certificate?"

Liz looked at Maggie as though she had lost all patience with her. "You know Helen Bordanowitz?"

Maggie nodded.

"The way I understand it, Helen Bordanowitz used to go to Port Richmond High School, and she had the gym locker next to Catherine Usherer—whoever that is —and one day when Catherine Usherer wasn't looking, Helen Bordanowitz stole it. Understand?"

Maggie felt her heart pounding. As Liz pushed her into the crowded bar she still couldn't understand how Liz had gotten the card.

Sean reached down for the lever to move the car seat back. "We should've gone to the Red Pub."

"Yeah," Dennis agreed.

"I find drinking beer in a car very demoralizing, do you know that?"

"I find everything demoralizing," Dennis said.

"Me too."

Dennis shifted his position so his right arm hung out the window. He leaned his head back, and the little holes in the roof upholstery caught his eye. It was the first time he had noticed what a car roof was made of. Plastic. Plastic with a lot of small holes in it.

"She really drives me up a wall," Sean said, lighting a cigarette.

"Who?"

"She drives me up a wall," he repeated. "Liz."

"Oh."

"The whole sex thing does," Sean continued. "Do you ever think about it? I mean *really* think about it?"

"Sure."

"I don't think you do."

"I do," Dennis insisted. There was a long silence, then he added, "I don't have as much experience as you, I guess."

Sean blew a puff of smoke toward his reflection in the side mirror. "I think our whole society is screwed up."

"Me too."

"I've thought about it a lot, and I think human beings should do what Nature wants them to do. You know what I mean?"

"What do you mean?"

"I mean, Nature wants us to breathe air. Right? We breathe air. Not water. *Air*. If somebody stops us from breathing air, we die. That's how my mind works. If I don't know what to do, I ask what does Nature want me to do. Does that sound nutty?"

"No."

Sean straightened up behind the wheel. That's

what he liked about Dennis. He could tell him whatever was on his mind. Tell him any ridiculous thought that ran through his head, and he at least tried to understand.

"Nature gives us a diaphragm and lungs and an air tube. The whole process goes on whether we want respiration or not. You can hold your breath, but all you do is pass out. Right? Nature forces you to do things, don't you think?"

"It sure does," Dennis said.

"Now. This sex thing. We never used to be hung up like this. Nature doesn't give little kids problems except when there's some kind of an accident—like that eight-year-old South American girl that had a baby. But that's practically a mutation. Right?"

"Right."

"But now Nature starts doing things. The hormones start rolling and those old testicles start producing and all the rest of it—like breathing. You don't go around asking for it. It happens. It happened to me when I was twelve."

"Fourteen," Dennis said softly.

"Fourteen?" Sean asked with surprise.

"Yes." Dennis sounded defensive now.

"You *sure?*"

"Of course I'm sure."

Dennis pulled his arm in from outside and sank lower in the seat.

Sean went on. "Now, I don't care what anyone says, Nature arranged it so that we have the equipment. And the need. So we'd better find a way, or we're going to do something as bad as suffocating. If you ask me, that's why there're so many sickies in the world. Everybody gets suffocated as teenagers."

Dennis thought for a moment. "I heard you can get married in India when you're ten years old."

"No kidding?"

Sean thought for a moment. "What kind of a honeymoon can you have in the fourth grade?"

They both roared with laughter, and Dennis kept slapping his knee.

"Did you ever have a wet dream?" Sean asked.

"A couple."

"They're funny, aren't they?"

"Yes."

Dennis picked up a pack of matches from the dashboard. He tore one of them out and began to pull apart the end.

"She's afraid of getting pregnant," Sean said. He took the pack of matches out of Dennis' hand and lit another cigarette.

"What?" Dennis asked.

"Liz." Sean put the pack of matches back on the dashboard. "She says she loves me and wants to have sex, but she's afraid."

"Oh . . ."

"Is that all you've got to say?"

Dennis knew he wasn't good at talking about things like this—even to a friend like Sean. He wasn't sure at all how he felt about anything, and it always made him say something silly.

"Sometimes I wonder . . ." Dennis started.

"What?" Sean asked.

"Do you think girls care about sex the way we do?"

English Honors 12 H 1   Dean Collins
Homework   Register 71-8

   Assignment: Compose a poem which you
          feel reflects a social problem of
   our time.

There was a young maid from Brazil,
who depended each time on the pill,
It all went just right
Except Mardi gras night
And now there's one more mouth to fill.

6

December 1, Friday

DEAR SEAN,

    I am writing this at the Red Pub Inn. Maggie and I came here because I wanted to see you, but you didn't show up. I hope you don't mind that I'm writing on these paper place mats, but that was all the waiter would give me—plus a pencil and an envelope. I'm just as glad you didn't show up because my horoscope said Saturday would be my lucky day. You'll be reading this on Saturday, and I've got my fingers crossed.

    I was very angry with you for treating me the way you did, which is why I didn't want to speak to you on the phone. I sent you a lot of notes last year in school, but they were just kidding. This letter is serious, and I hope you won't mind if it comes out awkwardly.

    After I didn't talk to you this week, I looked up my horoscope.

TAURUS (April 21—May 21) HOROSCOPE FOR NOVEMBER—THE PECULIAR SIDE OF YOUR PERSONALITY IS MAKING YOU EXTREMELY SENSITIVE. IF YOU FIND YOURSELF ALONE, DON'T BLAME ANYONE BUT YOURSELF. YOU ARE INTELLIGENT, YOU HAVE INITIATIVE, BUT YOUR LOVE LIFE

WILL HAVE ITS UPS AND DOWNS ESPECIALLY IF YOU CAN'T
CONTROL YOUR EGOTISTICAL TENDENCIES. YOUR ELEMENT:
The Earth. LUCKY DAY: Saturdays.

*After I read this, I began to wonder if I was fair to
you. I still think what you want me to do is wrong.
But I should have discussed it with you before things
got as far as they did. Please, Sean, don't tear up this
letter until you've finished reading it. Please. I love
you, Sean. Please finish reading it.*

*This whole letter sounds so stupid I feel psycho, but
I've got to finish. I think the problem is you don't
know me. You think I'm stronger than I am because
nothing seems to bother me on the outside. That's not
true. I'm always saying something sarcastic, but I
don't mean it that way. Don't you think I ever cry? I
cried for half the night when you called me a pain in
the ass.*

*Rod Gittens and Don McHugh gave Maggie and me a
ride here last week, so if anybody tells you they saw
us in their car, that's all it was. I just don't feel like
ending up the way Rod's girl friend did, having an
abortion.*

*I need you, Sean, more than anything in the world.
The only time I feel alive is when I'm with you. Even
when we fight, I don't care as long as we make up.
My stepfather thinks I have loose morals. He thinks a
lot of dirty things, and he's turned my mother against
me. She used to stick up for me, but now she does
whatever he says. I think she's scared of him. Either
that, or I'm no good and not worth worrying about.
I'm glad my father is dead because if he could see
what she married, he'd be ashamed. They don't trust
me at all. I've known for months my mother goes
through my pocketbook. I tape a piece of thread on
the hinges so I can tell when she does it. She must be
looking for goof balls or birth-control pills. I feel like*

asking our family doctor for a prescription just to shock the hell out of all of them. My mother never used to be that way. Only the last year or so, since she married him. I think he's oversexed. He's always got it on his mind. I can tell the way he looks at me. Just because they're doing whatever they're doing doesn't mean they have to think you and I are. I'm getting tired of getting blamed for things. I happen to think I have very high standards. I think you do too—in spite of yourself. Do you know my mother asked if you took dope? They think those things about everybody. Except the people at the Country Club. They think they're going to get in there, but I don't.

They were like that before I started going out with you. I wanted you to know that so you'll know how important you are in my life. Sean, if I lose you, I won't have anybody. If Maggie knew I was saying that, she would be hurt. But it's true. I like her a lot, but it's different between you and me. And I don't mean just physical. That's why I'm writing this letter. Damn these place mats! You're my whole world. I just sent Maggie to the jukebox to play "You're My World" six times. It's driving everybody else mad, but it says exactly what I feel about you, and I don't care about them. You are my world, my everything, Sean, and I'll do anything to have things good between us.

When we first went out, remember all the fun we had? You didn't even kiss me on the first date. I mean, we didn't even think about it because the Travis 4th of July picnic was so much fun. Remember, you won the doll for me at the bazaar? And then when you did kiss me the first time, it was nice and natural. You probably don't remember exactly, because I know boys forget that kind of thing. Girls don't. You kissed me on the sidewalk on July 5th at 10:30 at night. Just a little one. And then you kissed me at the door. I knew somebody was watching from upstairs. It was either my mother or stepfather, but I didn't care. I didn't care if the whole world saw you kiss me. I just want to remind you because you seemed to be very happy with me then and we weren't doing very much.

When you got the car, you used to park in front at night, and my mother started complaining it wasn't right. We weren't kissing all the time. We did a lot of talking. Remember how you used to think about blowing your head off with a gun? I can hear you saying I'm blaming the whole thing on you, and I'm not. I know I'm the one that said we'd better not park in front anymore because my mother and stepfather were always so dirty-minded. That was the only reason I wanted to park at Marine Beach. I got sick of the cross-examination. I used to go to bed with a lump in my stomach.

We had wonderful nights at the beach, and I'm not saying we didn't. I just think we started going too far. We went further and further on each date, and you expected to always get as far each time, and if I stopped you, you'd say I was being mean. Did you think I wanted to stop? I want to have sex with you. I've often thought what it would be like! You think it's been so easy for me? We don't have any fun now when we go out. We used to enjoy the evening and think about kissing at the end of it. Now I can tell by looking at you you can't wait for the movie or miniature-golf game to be finished so we can go park. You think about what's going to happen at the end of the evening before it gets started. And you've got me worrying about how I'm going to stop us from going too far, so no wonder we don't have fun anymore. No wonder I'm a pain in the ass.

Maggie says she's got to leave, so I want to finish and get this in your mailbox on the way home. It's very simple. I want you, but I think we should be engaged *first. I want to be your wife and have children and live with you the rest of my life. But I don't want to do everything now when we should wait. You wouldn't respect me if I did. You say you would, but I know you wouldn't. I love you. I love you. I love you. Please read this seriously and try to see my side. I want to do what you want. I want you to be happy. I don't think that is egotistical. I really don't. I may sound unreasonable now, but I love you. That's the only way I can say it. If you leave me, I'll want to die.*

Love,

Elizabeth Carstensen

December Something
the very, very dumpy Cafeteria

Liz;

I just saw Dennis. He got a pass from
Problems in American Democracy and asked
me to go to the G. O. dance.
    Would you mind if I said _yes_ ?
Maybe Sean will still answer your letter.

                Love,
                    XXX
                Maggie

P. S. If not, why don't you go with
    someone else? Half the boys in the
    school want to go with you, but
    Dennis is the only one who'd ask me.

                    Ha!

The General Organization.
of
Benjamin Franklin High School
announces the

WINTER STARLIGHT DANCE

Stag or Drag

Saturday, December 18

G.O. Members $1.00 Non-G.O. $1.50

7

"YOU LOOK VERY PRETTY, Liz," Mrs. Palladino said at the entrance to her daughter's room.

"Thank you, Mother."

She went to Liz and kissed her on the cheek. "What time is the young man picking you up?"

"In a few minutes."

"That's nice," Mrs. Palladino said. She clasped her hands in front of her, then sat on Liz's bed. "I see you've moved it."

"What?"

"The Madonna."

Liz looked over at the small desk in her room. The statue stood on top of a pile of old horoscope magazines.

"Something on your mind, Mother?"

Mrs. Palladino grinned. She searched for just the right words. "Nothing really. It's that I want you to know we've noticed an improvement in your attitude since you've stopped seeing the Collins boy."

"You don't say."

"Your father told me how pleased he is you've been halfway friendly. I appreciate it very much. He may not be the most patient and congenial person in the world, but he wants you to like him, and he's trying in his own way."

Liz felt that if she didn't get out of the room, she'd say something she'd be sorry about later. "Excuse me, Mom."

"Of course." Mrs. Palladino smiled weakly.

Liz went into the bathroom where two fluorescent lights lined the medicine-cabinet mirror. She concentrated on finishing her makeup, trying to keep the pain she felt inside herself and not think about it—not let it into words as she'd done over and over during the last weeks. One tear formed, but she caught it with a tissue. She decided to concentrate on what her mother had just said. Anything to get her mind off Sean. Perhaps it *was* better at home now. In fact, she liked her mother to compliment her occasionally, even if it was for the wrong things. And her stepfather *had* seemed almost pleasant during dinner. She hadn't been overly friendly at the time, but she managed to smile, and apparently he had noticed.

Liz stood back a moment and looked at herself in the mirror on the closet door. They had let her get a new dress for the dance. She loved the blue color, the style. It was exactly what she had wanted. Even if she didn't feel too good inside, she was thankful the exterior worked out.

Mr. Palladino was in the living room when she came downstairs. He looked up. She smiled broadly and waited.

Mrs. Palladino hurried in from the kitchen drying her hands. "Doesn't she look lovely?"

Liz was annoyed that her mother had prompted.

"Too low-cut, isn't it?" Mr. Palladino went back to reading the newspaper.

"That's the style nowadays, isn't it, Liz?"

"Yes," Liz said.

Mr. Palladino looked up again. "Can't you cover yourself up a little?"

"No, I can't," Liz said quickly.

Mrs. Palladino sat down near her husband. She leaned toward him, almost pleading. "Tell Liz you think it's very attractive, dear."

"You asked me what I thought, and I told you."

"Thanks," Liz said. She wanted to run out of the room.

"I think it's too low-cut and too tight, and if you were my daughter, I wouldn't let you out of the house in it."

"I *am* your daughter," Liz screamed at him. She turned and headed for the hall.

The front doorbell rang. Mrs. Palladino came into the hall just as Liz was putting on her coat.

"Hello." Mrs. Palladino was embarrassed that Liz hadn't introduced her to the strange young man standing there. "I'm Liz's mother."

"Hello." The boy gave her a mocking smile.

Mrs. Palladino opened her mouth. She didn't quite know what to say.

Liz opened the front door and started out. The young man started to follow her.

"I don't believe I caught the gentleman's name," Mrs. Palladino said.

"Rod," Liz said. "The gentleman's name is Rod."

She slammed the door.

A few flakes of snow had already fallen. Liz felt better after a moment in the fresh air. When they reached the car, she turned to look back at the house. The snow had veiled the roof, changing it from brown to gray. The lawn was barren, and a few of the bushes near the entrance sparkled with their covering of ice. Her mother was looking out the living-room window, and she saw her step-father stand up and walk across the room. It was strange how the frost on the window distorted them both, twisted them.

Rod opened the car door for her. The seat was cold when she touched it, and the slam of the door made her aware of a throbbing in her head.

"What are you chewing?" Rod asked.

Liz's back hit the cold leather as the car started off. "Aspirin."

"You chew it?"

"Do you mind?"

They drove in silence for a few minutes. Then Liz regretted having turned her anger on someone who didn't deserve it. After all, she was the one who had called and asked him to take her to the dance.

"How's your job?" she asked.

"What?" he said nastily. She knew he was retaliating.

She moved closer and put her arm on his shoulder. "I'm sorry."

He smiled. "Light me a cigarette."

She pushed the dashboard lighter in as far as it could go. "What kind of therapy did you say you did?"

"Inhalation therapy."

"It sounds interesting."

"Not bad."

The lighter popped out, and Liz lit two cigarettes. She put one of them between his lips.

"I handle everything with the oxygen. Make sure the tanks are set up right. Regulate the liters per minute."

The windshield wipers made a rhythmic tapping which was getting on Liz's nerves. She tried to keep a smile on her face and look attentive, but she knew she wasn't doing a convincing job of it. Fortunately, Rod was concentrating on the snowy road.

"You read about that old lady they found half dead on Victory Boulevard a couple of nights ago?"

"No," Liz said.

"Well, anyway, I gave her oxygen, but she died. I saw her autopsy this morning. Right in there with the doctors. I see everything. Been at dozens of autopsies. This Dr. Conger down there lets me in on all the good stuff."

Liz was not sure what to answer or even if an answer was necessary. He had a habit of pausing after every sentence as though waiting for a response. His eyes were what gave him away, she decided. Everything else was perfect. But his eyes—they were the clue to how ugly he was inside.

"I've seen everything, believe me," he said.

"I'm sure."

"Everything except a dame dropping a baby. One doctor's lining that up as soon as he can. I give them oxygen in maternity before they go to delivery. They scream like they were dying, and the thing's not even coming out yet. I'm looking forward to seeing one all the way through."

Liz turned on the radio and waited for it to warm up. She had tried being polite, but now she was sorry she'd ever called him.

"The Doc says he can't let me watch until we get one on charity. Private cases are restricted, but they pack the delivery room for the charity ones."

"Where's Don?" Liz asked.

The radio had come on too loud. He reached his hand over to turn it down, then he left his hand on her knee. "He's got something going for him tonight."

"He won't be at the dance?"

"No." He looked at her, and his lips broke into a smile. "He could've fixed me up too."

"I'm sorry."

"Don't be sorry," he said, squeezing her knee. "We're going to have just as good a time, aren't we?"

8

MAGGIE LOOKED ALMOST BEAUTIFUL sitting beside Dennis as they bounced along on the hard seats of the bus. As he looked at her, he realized she had lost quite a bit of weight. She wasn't thin, but all of her pudginess was gone. She smiled widely at him as they got off the bus.

They walked toward the sound of music coming from the school. It had stopped snowing, and a full moon showed itself from behind a cloud. It practically made up for the bumpy bus ride, Dennis felt.

"Is Sean coming?" Maggie asked.

"Nope."

"Liz is going with Rod Gittens, you know."

Dennis almost slipped on a patch of ice. "What's she going with him for?"

Maggie thought for a moment. "I think she wants to punish herself."

Dennis helped her up the steps of the main entrance. "I hope Sean and her get back together," he said.

"So do I," Maggie agreed.

Mr. Zamborsky was in a classroom near the boys' gym, guarding coats. Dennis dug around in the rear closet and finally found an empty hook.

"Good evening, Mr. Zamborsky," Maggie said.

Mr. Zamborsky nodded. "Don't leave any valuables. I'm not responsible for stolen property, you understand?"

"Yes, Mr. Zamborsky," Dennis said.

Wwwwwrrrrrrrrrrrrrr! Mr. Zamborsky blew the whistle around his neck. He darted by Maggie and Dennis and started to scream down the hall, "No smoking in the building! You kids at the end of the hall! Do you hear me? No smoking!"

WWWWWWWWWrrrrrrrrrrrr!

Maggie took Dennis' arm as they walked down the steps to the boys' gym. The two large entrance doors were wide open, and Pierre Jefferson was overseeing the ticket taking.

"Hello, Pierre," Maggie said.

"Hello."

"I enjoyed your viewpoint in Tuesday's history class."

Pierre smiled and smoothed his hair. "Thank you."

"*What* viewpoint?" Dennis whispered.

"He reported on Taxation without Representation."

They paused for a moment inside the gym. The band was playing a slow number, and everything was lighted a deep amber. A large mirrored ball hung from the ceiling, sending speckles of light over the dancers and walls as it revolved.

"Would you like to dance?" Dennis asked.

Maggie smiled. "Yes."

He felt glorious holding her in his arms. What a difference, he thought. What a difference.

"Your dress is beautiful," he said.

"Thank you. It's Grecian."

"Oh?"

"The style. Grecian."

He thought it a miraculous improvement over the one she had worn to the movies on their first date. She was like an entirely different girl.

"The decorations are fascinating, don't you think?" Maggie remarked.

"Sort of."

"There's Miss Blair over there."

Maggie noticed a number of girls look at Dennis. He did look good tonight, compared to what he used to look like. He never wore the baggy green sweater anymore.

"I like your suit."

Dennis grinned. "Thank you."

"It's new, isn't it?"

"I got it at Hagen's Men's Store. They have a clothing club where you pay two dollars a week for thirty weeks with a raffle every month, so if you win, you don't have to wait thirty weeks."

"That's a good idea," Maggie said, not knowing what on earth he was talking about.

Then she remembered the shocking yellow shirt he had worn the first night he took her to that disgusting show. Imagine! Pygmies chopping the head off a water buffalo! Sean must have influenced his taste in clothes, she decided. Tonight he was actually dashing.

"Hello, Miss Blair," Maggie said as a woman with teased white hair danced past.

"Hello, Maggie," Miss Blair said. She smiled ecstatically in Pierre Jefferson's arms. "Hello, Dennis."

Dennis and Maggie stopped dancing a moment as Miss Blair did a couple of special spins and a dip. Several other couples cheered her on. They usually did that for Miss Blair because she chaperoned all the dances. She always got out on the floor. If it wasn't with Pierre Jefferson, it was some other junior or senior.

"*Go*, Miss Blair," someone yelled out.

Liz went to the girls' room as soon as they arrived. She brushed a few drops of melted snow from her hair and touched up her eye makeup. Then she tried to flatten out a small wrinkle in her dress. Everything had to be perfect.

"What the hell took you so long?" Rod asked when she returned.

She looked at him and decided not to answer. She put her arm in his. "Come on."

"Hi, Liz," Pierre Jefferson said.

She nodded back. It was strange the way Pierre wouldn't look at Rod. At least he pretended not to look, she thought. That was what everyone was doing.

"Let's dance," she said.

He put his arm around her, and she moved very close to him. There wasn't a boy in that gym who was better looking than Rod Gittens. That was what mattered. She wasn't sitting home. She wasn't in mourning over anybody. Not anybody.

"Hello, Liz."

Liz smiled when she saw Miss Blair dance by with Frankie Piconia.

"Hello, Miss Blair."

"Who's that?" Rod whispered in her ear.

"A teacher."

"You're kidding!"

Liz moved her left hand higher on his shoulder and stroked the back of his neck when she noticed Miss Blair continuing to stare. He was causing precisely the kind of reaction she wanted. She wanted it to get around. Let them talk.

"Who're you looking for?" Rod asked.

"Nobody."

"You keep looking around the place."

"I'm just admiring the decorations."

The band stopped for a moment, then started again with a fast beat.

"Let's get a soda," he said, leading her off the floor. She enjoyed the way everyone stopped chattering when they came near. The crowd at the soda counter moved subtly to accommodate them. He was served immediately, and then he carried the sodas to a corner near the band.

"Hold them," he said.

She watched him take out a narrow silver flask from his jacket, unscrew the cap, and pour a bit of fluid into each of the paper cups. Then he screwed the top back on. "A little hundred-and-fifty proof—compliments of the hospital." He put the flask back into his inside pocket and took one of the paper cups. He raised it in a toast. "You look like a knockout, honey."

"Thank you," Liz said, tasting her drink suspiciously.

The two of them stood listening to the band.

"Did you ever see an autopsy?" he asked.

She could tell he was uncomfortable, and it wasn't only that the crowd was too young for him. He'd be uncomfortable anywhere after the first five minutes of strutting and crowing. Unless there was one wild kick after another, he didn't know what to do. It was always back to the same subject. Always something a little twisted.

"Did you ever see an autopsy?" he repeated.

Liz looked up at the revolving mirrored ball and deliberately let the light flashes hit her eyes. It was almost hypnotic, and for a moment she remembered the last time on the beach. She had almost forgotten about her astrology forecast that last night. There must have been some facet to it she had failed to interpret. She tried to remember, but only a few phrases came back. *PRAY TO THE MADONNA. YOU WILL BE PUNISHED FOR YOUR SINS . . . EVEN YOUR SINS OF OMISSION. YOU EMBRACE LIFE . . . YOU WILL SUFFER . . . ONE DAY YOU COULD MURDER. PRAY TO THE MADONNA. ON SUNDAYS PRAY TO THE MADONNA. PRAY. YOU COULD MURDER . . .*

"You know that?"

"I'm sorry," Liz said. "I couldn't hear you over the band."

"As soon as they cut open the chest, you can smell death. You just *smell* it," he told her.

"There's Liz."

"Where?" Maggie asked.

"Under the big paper star."

Maggie took Dennis' hand and dragged him across the floor. Liz saw her coming and started to wave.

"Hi, Liz."

Liz gave Maggie a hug and put up her cheek for
Dennis to kiss.

"You remember Rod?"

"Yes," Maggie said coldly.

Dennis shook hands with him. Then the four stood
looking at each other.

"You having a nice time?" Maggie asked.

Liz spoke in a monotone. "Rod was just telling me
how they do an autopsy."

"How *do* they?" Dennis asked. Maggie shot him a
look.

"Have you seen anyone interesting?" Liz asked with
a little wink.

Maggie looked into Liz's eyes to see if they were
talking about the same thing. She turned her head in
Rod's direction and said, "Definitely not."

"Come on, Liz," Rod said. "Let's dance."

Maggie watched them blend into the crowd. She
was fuirous about Rod's whole attitude. Without a
doubt, he was the most repulsive person she'd ever
met.

"He seems like a nice guy," Dennis said.

Maggie sighed. "What do you know?"

"I've got a right to my opinion."

Suddenly Maggie had an idea. At first she thought
it was a good one. Then she decided it'd be better to
forget it. Finally she couldn't resist.

"Where are you going?" Dennis asked.

"I'll be right back," Maggie called over her shoulder.

She headed for the main exit. Pierre and Miss Blair
were at the ticket table, and she broke into a slight
run so they wouldn't have a chance to snag her into
wasting a second. Perhaps Liz would hate her for
what she was going to do. That was the chance she
would have to take.

The phone booth on the third floor was occupied,
so she ran down a flight of stairs. The door marshal on
the second floor let her use the one there. Her hand
was shaking as she dialed the number.

"May I speak to Sean Collins, please?"

"Who is this?" a deep voice asked. Maggie knew it must be his father.

"Maggie Tobin."

"Just a minute. I'll see if he's in his room."

She wondered what he meant by "he'd see." Didn't he know if his own son was home? If Sean weren't there, she decided she'd try the Red Pub Inn.

"Hello?"

Maggie recognized the voice. "Sean, this is Maggie. I'm calling from the dance."

"Hello, Maggie," Sean said quietly.

"Sean, I don't want to butt in where I'm not wanted, but it's been weeks since you've spoken to Liz or me, and I had to find out what was wrong. I know you two had a fight, but you could've answered her letter and told her . . ."

"What letter?"

"The letter she left in your mailbox two Saturdays ago, written on place mats."

There was a moment of silence on the other end. Maggie waited for a response. "Sean?"

"I didn't get any letter."

"She put it in your mailbox. I saw her."

There was another pause.

"What'd she say in it?"

"She told me she apologized."

Maggie heard a click on the line as if someone had picked up an extension. "Do you have another phone in your house?" she asked. There was a second noise, and she could tell the line was closed again. "Do they spy on you in your own house?"

"They want me to bring my grades up."

"Your father?"

"Mainly."

"Could he have taken the letter?" Maggie asked.

"Look," Sean said, "where's Liz?"

"At the dance."

"I'll be right down."

Maggie tried to cry out before he hung up, but it

was too late. She wanted to tell him Liz was with
Rod Gittens. She fumbled through her purse for another dime, but all she found was two pennies. The
marshal near the door had no change, and by the
time she could get back to the gym to get a dime, she
knew Sean would have left.

The band was thunderous as Maggie pushed her
way through the mob of dancers. She looked around,
but the flashing lights were paralyzing. Finally Dennis found her.

"Where's Liz?"

Dennis wondered why she was so excited. "I don't
know. They went out the door."

Maggie started toward the exit, and Dennis hurried
after her. "Do you mind telling me what's going on?"

"Later."

In the hall outside the gym they passed Miss Blair
again. She was talking to Mr. Zamborsky. Maggie
checked the classroom with the coats first. The closet
was overflowing. All the desks were covered. Finally
she saw Liz's coat on a radiator near the window.

"She didn't leave."

Maybe Liz had followed her out before, thinking
she was going to the girls' room, Maggie thought. Rod
wasn't around, but he could be anyplace.

"Check the boys' room and let me know if Rod's in
there," Maggie ordered.

"But—" Dennis stopped himself. He saw there was
no point in arguing.

Maggie watched Dennis disappear down the stairs.
Then she started for the girls' room. She walked
several feet down the hall to where it turned. The
girls' room was at the far end of the hall. She saw a
marshal sitting outside one of the rooms.

"Did you see Liz Carstensen?" Maggie asked.

"She got long blond hair?"

"Yes."

"She went by with some guy."

She slowed down in order to think. They wouldn't
both be heading in the direction of the girls' room.

But something made her continue walking down the long hall. She'd been in that corridor many times before, going to and from classes, but for the first time she noticed the bizarre paintings that lined the walls. She never saw them when the halls were packed with kids pushing this way and that. In silence, the corridor was frightening.

Two girls from her gym class came toward her. She couldn't remember their names.

"Did you see Liz Carstensen?" Maggie asked.

The two girls started to laugh.

Maggie was annoyed. "What's so funny?"

"We saw her," one girl said. "She's in the art room."

The other girl hurriedly added, "But the only thing she's drawing is a crowd."

The girls' laughter reverberated in the hall. Maggie quickened her pace. She stopped at the open door of the room.

"Liz?" she whispered.

She heard a noise on the other side of the room. When no one answered, she flicked the lights on.

"Put them off," Rod yelled. He had Liz against the rear wall.

Maggie swallowed. Her throat had gone dry, and she could hardly speak. "Are you all right, Liz?"

"Yes."

"Are you sure?"

"I said *Yes*."

Maggie felt hurt as she reached her hand back up to the light switch. She flicked it off and then started back down the hall. She didn't know what to do.

"You turn me on, honey."

Liz laughed and turned her head to see if anyone else had stopped at the open door to look in.

"Really turn me on."

It had gone just as she planned. She had picked that room because all the gossipy girls would have to pass by it at one point or another. And she had made certain that enough of the worst rumor mongers had seen them go in.

"Let's go back," Liz said. She tried to move away, but he held her.

"We'll stay awhile." He smiled at her and pressed his lips on hers. She made another attempt to move, but he tightened his grip.

"Easy," he whispered.

A few minutes before, she had been in possession of the situation. All she had needed to do was flutter her eyelashes, and she had her way. But now she wanted him to stop, and he wouldn't.

"Please stop, Rod."

"You feel like dynamite, baby."

"Please."

"Baby, you don't turn dynamite on and off like a radio. You know better than that."

She was worried now that she was no longer in control. His hands seemed to be all over. He had managed to open the zipper on the back of her dress. She could hit him—maybe push him with all her strength. She began to tremble.

"It's all right, honey."

She could scream, she knew. They'd hear her. Any sound echoed in the halls. At least the marshals would hear. All she had to do was *do* it. Scream at the top of her lungs.

"Stop," she pleaded.

"Real easy, honey."

She felt along the wall with her left hand, desperately trying to find a grip and to pull herself away from him. All she felt was the rough cork surface of a bulletin board. She was ready to scream when her fingers touched metal. Small smooth circles of cold metal. She tried to work one of them free. She couldn't pry it loose at first, but finally she got her fingernail under and lifted it out. She turned it around carefully so the short pointed end was ready.

"Please stop," she begged.

The weight of his body was crushing. "We're just beginning," he said.

With a sudden thrust she drove the tack into his neck. Instantly he yelled and bolted upright, pulling the tack out. He stared disbelievingly at the blood on his hand and then slapped her across the face.

She blinked against the flood of light that followed. It was a moment before she knew it was Sean at the doorway. He stood there glaring, Maggie standing behind him. Suddenly he strode toward them, grabbed Rod by the back of his collar, and lifted him up. For a second it looked as though he was holding a rag doll.

When Rod recovered, he sprang to his full height, knocking Sean against the wall. He reached into his jacket pocket and took out a long thin leather case. From its interior emerged a shiny piece of metal.

Sean changed his position slowly, edging his back against the wall. He didn't blink, didn't turn his head, just kept his eyes glued on the polished scalpel that moved toward him.

"Stop it!" Miss Blair screamed from the doorway.

Rod held his attacking position but shifted in the direction of the windows so he could see her.

Miss Blair kept her distance, sizing him up. She stared at him until finally his expression softened.

"I'll get the police," she threatened.

Rod laughed. "What for?" He looked at Liz and then Sean. Then he relaxed the position of the scalpel. "I was just going to give my friend a little manicure. Right, Sean, baby?" He returned the instrument to its narrow case and put it back in his pocket. Slowly he moved toward the rear door.

"Nice seeing you, honey." He glared at Liz a moment. "We'll do it again sometime. Soon."

Miss Blair watched him open the door. "I'm going to report this!" she said.

Rod halted, turned, and looked at her. "Go back to that fag dance, you old pig."

He slammed the door behind him.

9

SHE WAS AFRAID Sean would have driven off by the time she got her coat and ran out to the street, but she saw the car parked at the corner. She slowed down as she got closer and strained to see his face behind the flapping windshield wipers. He rolled down his window, brushing off a ridge of snow so it wouldn't fall inside.

"What do you want?" he asked.

She thought if she could find the right words he'd at least be willing to park somewhere and talk. He would have driven off if he had wanted to be through with her. Then she realized it didn't matter so much what she said as long as it gave him a chance to tell her the way he felt.

"I'm sorry," she said.

"You're sorry?" he bellowed at her. "How the hell do you think I feel walking in and finding you with the clothes half off your back?"

"I . . ."

"Maybe hoods are more your type." He stared straight ahead, refusing to look at her. She waited. When he took a deep breath and relaxed his grip on the steering wheel, she knew the worst was over.

"Get in," he said.

She hurried to the other side of the car. He leaned across and unlocked the door for her. They drove off in silence.

She thought the car would never warm up and

leaned forward to rub her hands near the heater. By the time they arrived at the beach she finally felt warm. She wiped a circle on the windshield to see where on the shore road they had parked. A few hundred yards away was the light of the only telephone booth at Marine Park, and it gave her her bearings.

She waited for him to speak.

"I didn't get your letter, you know. My father must have taken it."

She looked at him and knew they both were thinking the same thing—it wasn't his not getting the letter that was the problem.

"What are we going to do?" she asked.

"How do I know?" He slumped down in his seat with a flash of hurt in his eyes.

"When you didn't call, I didn't want to be alive anymore. You were on my mind every minute," she said. "On the way to school I found myself looking in the direction of where you live. Blocks and blocks away, but I couldn't help wondering if you knew the way I missed you."

He looked at her and wanted to reach out and touch her, but somehow he couldn't. As if she had read his mind, she moved her hand and touched his. She moved closer to him, and he turned to hold her. The softness of her cheek against his reminded him of how much he had missed her. He lowered his head and let his lips lightly touch hers, wanting to promise her that would be enough. In a few minutes they were back to the same old point again.

She turned sideways, resting her right arm on the dashboard.

"Is it that you think I won't respect you?" Sean asked quietly. "I'll still respect you. We love each other. I need you, Liz."

He moved toward her. She felt so miserable inside. She wanted him just as much as he wanted her. He had begun to kiss her when a car came roaring by, its headlights flooding the interior. A drunken voice yelled out, "*Save a piece for me!*" Then the car was gone.

"I think you'd better take me home," Liz said slowly, moving away.

Sean's face hardened as he tapped the accelerator to make certain the motor was still running. He put the car in gear. As it moved along the road a thumping noise started.

"What is it?" asked Liz.

"Damn!" Sean opened the door, and a blast of cold air swept in. "A flat." He slammed the door, leaving her alone.

She sat quietly staring at the frost pictures on the windshield. It reminded her of her mother. The way she had watched through the living-room window when Rod had put her in the car.

A chill ran through her as she opened the door and stepped out on the road.

"Where're you going?" Sean asked as he jacked up the back of the car.

"I've got to call home. They wanted me back at midnight."

She headed down the road toward the light of the telephone booth. She kept her head lowered to watch for patches of ice. Off to the left, the winter sea crashed in giant waves, and ripples of ice marked the tide lines.

She managed to get a dime in the phone without taking off her gloves. While she waited for someone to answer, she blew against the window of the booth and watched the intricate design that formed.

"Hello, Mom?"

"Where are you, Liz?"

Liz was glad to hear her voice. "I'm going to be a little late."

"But it's twelve o'clock now."

There was a shuffling in the background, then her stepfather's voice.

"You're late."

Liz was even glad to hear him. If he only knew

how much she wanted to be home instead of in that freezing phone booth.

"We had a flat," Liz said. "It's a bit complicated, but I had a fight with the boy that took me to the dance ..." Liz slowed her voice, then stopped. She felt she was saying all the wrong things.

"Get home here!"

The tone of his voice made her heart sink.

"Do you hear me, you little tramp?"

Liz froze. Slowly she removed the receiver from her ear and looked at it disbelievingly. Without a word, she put it back on the hook.

The door of the booth jammed. She tugged at it, and it flew open. On the way back to the car she kept her head high in the wind.

"Everything all right?" Sean called over the whine of the wind. He was tightening the spare into place.

"Yes," she said.

She got into the car and sat motionless. She felt absolutely and utterly alone. It was as if her mind had suddenly gone blank.

"Go to hell," she said under her breath—that was what she should have told her stepfather. What could he do? Punch her when she got home? Kick her? He wouldn't dare lay a hand on her, she knew, or she'd have him arrested. Let them both scream their heads off. She wouldn't even hear them because she was in another world millions of miles away. Another galaxy. Then, in the next moment, she was frightened. She didn't really have a world of her own. All she was certain of was that she didn't belong in theirs.

She heard the trunk slam shut. Finally Sean swung into the front seat next to her and wiped his face with his sleeve. He rubbed his hands near the heater for a few moments and then noticed the expression on Liz's face.

"Something the matter?"

"No."

She looked at him. She knew she had been wrong. She was no longer frightened about building the world in which she wanted to live. The start had already been made.

"I'm not in a hurry to go home anymore," she said. "Not anymore."

part two/the hamburger

April Fools Day
Ha!

Liz!

What's happened to you and Sean lately?
Dennis and I hardly ever see you two
anymore. Is anything wrong? I called
you 5 times last week, and you only
called me once. Aren't you glad the
winter's over?

I got a 98 in the physics midterm. I'm
the only one who knew what a pi-meson
was. Even Pierre Jefferson was impressed.
Send me a note from gym, O.K.?

Love,
Maggie

P.S. Are you going
shopping soon for a
prom dress? Call me!

April 2

Liz!!!

Why didn't you call me? The prom is only _days_ away. I've really got to get a dress. Can you meet me after eighth period tomorrow? I want to go to Garbergs or the Teen Shoppe. The Teen Shoppe has a sale.

Where have you been ????

Maggie

P.S. Is anything wrong?

Pierre ⟶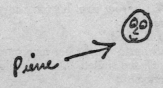

10

"CAN I HELP YOU, young ladies?"

Liz hated the saleswoman on sight. Her wrinkled powder-white face peeked out from under platinum bangs. Worst of all her eyelids were painted with metallic gold liner, so every time she blinked it was like flash bulbs going off.

"I want to look at a dress. *For the prom,*" Maggie said.

"Oh," said the woman, "you're from the high school."

"Yes."

"Right this way. We have some elegant frocks for you. Elegant."

Maggie chatted with the saleswoman as they moved through the racks of clothes, but Liz was silent. Maggie had actually buzzed from the moment they left school the whole way to The Teen Shoppe. Liz hadn't listened to half of what she had said, but it was innocuous enough to make a simple nod here and there a sufficient response.

The saleswoman gestured to a wall full of hanging dresses. "This is your size. It's too bad you didn't get here last week."

"Why?" Liz asked.

The saleswoman caught her tone immediately. "Selection, dear," she smiled. "There would have been a larger selection."

"Now all you've got is leftovers?" Liz snapped.

"Tell me, dear," the woman said, "are you shopping for a dress too?"

"Not here," Liz replied.

"You're not?" asked Maggie.

"No!" Liz despised the way the saleswoman was looking at her. "This stuff looks crappy anyway."

The saleswoman reached a hand up and touched her right eyelid. "The dressing room is *there* if you wish to try anything on."

"Thank you," Maggie said meekly.

The woman started to walk away. "One dress at a time."

"That's all she usually wears," Liz said. "One dress at a time."

The woman halted. "I mean in the dressing room. Only take in one dress at a time."

"Afraid we'll steal one?" Liz asked.

"Of course not." The woman smiled, then walked on.

Maggie waited a moment for an explanation. Then she put her pocketbook down on a chair and decided to wait until Liz offered one. Maggie started going through the racks, but she was so upset at how nasty Liz had been to the saleswoman she couldn't concentrate. She even had trouble reading the price tags. Finally she had to say something.

"Is something wrong, Liz? You sounded angry with the saleslady."

"Nothing," Liz said. She began to look through the dresses along with Maggie. Then she added, "I'm pregnant."

"What?"

"Pregnant!" Liz repeated.

Maggie turned to see if the saleswoman had heard, but she was busy taking inventory of a rack of shoes. Maggie continued to look through the dresses. She didn't know what to say.

"Are you *sure*?"

"I know."

"How?"

"How?" Liz repeated, mimicking Maggie's astonishment. "Because I haven't had my period for two months, and I puke in the mornings. That's how!"

Maggie took one of the dresses off the rack and held it helplessly in her hands.

"The lace neck is beautiful on that one," the saleswoman said. She was several yards away, but her voice pealed out clearly. "Why don't you try it on? There's nothing like a high neck. Dignified and elegant. Elegant!"

Maggie nodded to the saleswoman and turned back to Liz. "Maybe it's something else. Some kind of intestinal virus—"

Liz cut her short. "I haven't been exposed to intestinal *virus!*"

"Come in the dressing room," Maggie whispered.

She pulled open the curtain of the cubicle. The sliding hooks on top made a rattling noise, and they both turned to see the saleswoman still staring from the main counter. Liz stuck her tongue out and flung the curtains closed.

"I don't know what to say," Maggie whispered.

"Just try the dress on." Liz turned Maggie around and helped her with a zipper.

"I didn't know . . ." Maggie turned back around. Liz stared at her for a moment and then had to look away.

"Did you tell him?" Maggie asked.

"No."

"Your mother?"

Liz sighed with exasperation. "I didn't tell anybody. I'm telling *you.*" She helped Maggie get her dress off over her head and handed her the new one.

"We have that same style in yellow," a voice drifted in from outside.

Liz jerked open the curtain to see the saleslady standing outside holding a yellow dress.

"Isn't it pretty?"

Maggie held the white dress in front of her so no

one else in the store would see her in her slip. "Very pretty."

"Yeah," Liz agreed. "But it's more gold than yellow, wouldn't you say? Sort of the same shade as your eyeliner."

The woman held the dress at arm's length. "Why, perhaps you're right."

"A gaudy gold," Liz said.

"An *elegant* gold," the woman said.

Liz took hold of the curtain and flung it shut again. Maggie got her arms caught in the sleeves of the new dress, and Liz had to guide it for her.

"Hold still," Liz insisted as she helped smooth out the folds Maggie took a close look at Liz's eyes and saw how red they were. And her fingers were trembling too. Suddenly Maggie felt tears running out of her own eyes.

"For Christ's sake, don't *you* cry," Liz said.

"I'm sorry."

"Just stop."

"I think you've got to tell Sean."

Liz practically screamed at her. "I didn't ask what the hell you thought!" She flung open the curtain and saw the saleslady glaring in their direction. "Come out and make believe you're looking at yourself in the mirror. That bleached blond snoop is getting swollen eyeballs watching us."

Maggie forced a smile in the direction of the saleswoman and hurried to a three-way set of mirrors.

"You look lovely," the saleslady called, taking a step toward them.

"You can just stay there," Liz yelled. "My friend likes privacy when picking out clothes."

The saleslady stopped. "Is she *crying?*" she asked, her voice modulating an octave higher.

"It's a sentimental occasion," Liz said.

"Oh."

"We'll call *you*," Liz added.

The woman hung motionless for a moment. Finally she backed away.

"Don't stain the dress," she said, returning to the main counter.

Maggie took a tissue and started to dry her eyes. She felt horrible as she looked at her reflection echoing in the mirrors. And the neck of the dress was so tight—practically choking her.

"I've got it worked out," Liz said. She took the tissue and wiped a tear from Maggie's cheeks.

Maggie took a deep breath and swallowed hard.

"Are you finished crying?" Liz asked.

Maggie finally formed the words. "What are you going to do?"

"Give me a smile," Liz insisted.

"I can't smile."

"Come on."

"Liz ..."

"Come *on*."

Maggie felt foolish at the way Liz was babying her. Finally she had to smile.

"That's better."

"Liz ..."

"That lace collar looks like cheap surgical gauze," Liz said, adjusting the sleeves. Then she whispered, "I'm getting rid of it."

For a moment Maggie didn't understand what Liz meant. She thought she was talking about the lace, but she couldn't mean getting rid of the material. She finally understood.

Liz continued the pretense of admiring Maggie's dress so the saleslady wouldn't barge over. "Elegant!" Liz bellowed sarcastically. Then she lowered her voice.

"Stop shaking."

"I can't," Maggie said.

"I'll need your help."

"Liz ..."

"*Can I count on you?*"

Maggie looked away for a moment. She didn't want to believe it was happening. Then somehow she managed a nod.

"How much money do you have?" asked Liz.

The question took Maggie by surprise. She stuttered for a moment.

"About thirty-eight dollars. And they gave me twenty-five for a prom dress."

Liz did some calculations in silence.

"Haven't you told anybody?" Maggie asked. "Anybody besides me?"

"Yes."

"Who?"

"Rod."

"Rod Gittens!"

Liz turned away and looked at herself in the mirror. "Thirty-eight dollars," she repeated.

"Liz, what are you going to do?"

Liz turned back to Maggie. "You get the dress."

"But . . ."

"We're going to need it."

Liz looked into the mirror again.

Maggie went to the chair where she had left her pocketbook. She took out a bank book and opened it. "That's it. Thirty-eight dollars.". .

"Plus my forty-one. Me with forty-one and you with thirty-eight. How the hell am I going to get an abortion on seventy-nine bucks!" Liz asked.

"Are you having a money problem?" the saleswoman inquired as she strode toward them.

"No," Maggie said. The woman hung over them a moment. She stroked daintily at her lashes, as if she had gotten a piece of dust in her eyes. "Perhaps you'd prefer to charge it," she smiled. "Would you like that?"

11

"SEAN'S BEEPING THE HORN," Mrs. Palladino called out.

Liz rushed downstairs. She found her mother waiting in the hall with a strange smile on her face.

"I'll be back in an hour," Liz said. "We're going for a drive."

"Liz," Mrs. Palladino said, "I want you to know how much I appreciate the way you've been acting lately."

Liz had her hand on the doorknob before the words got through to her. "What do you mean?"

Mrs. Palladino smiled. "You've got to excuse me. I sometimes pick the wrong words. But tonight at dinner—I don't know if you noticed it, but it's the first time you've discussed your plans with us. We're very excited about the prom. Just as much as you." She lowered her voice so her husband wouldn't hear. "He was very pleased you asked his advice on where to go after the dance. Couldn't you tell? He simply beamed. The Holiday Club. He's taken me there several times. It is lovely."

"Do you think he'll let me stay out late?" Liz asked, opening the door.

"I'm sure he will, dear. After all, you only have one senior prom," Mrs. Palladino said. "It's a once-in-a-lifetime affair."

"It certainly is," Liz said, slamming the door behind her.

Maggie made straight for her room and threw herself on the bed. Her head was spinning, and she tried to take her mind off what had happened. The bed-spread beneath her was striated with ridges of black thread, and she began counting the rows from the edge of the bed to the spot where her head lay. A silly noisemaker caught her eye. It hung limply on the wall, a souvenir from a basketball game she had gone to as a freshman. Then she focused on a picture of her mother on the dresser, an old snapshot of an awkward-looking young girl smiling bashfully at the camera.

That had been the worst. All the lying she had to do at dinner. Her parents wanted to know where the new dress was, and she had told them she left it at the store for alterations. Then they wanted to know when she would pick it up. She told them *soon*. It was getting to be one lie after another, and she had never been very good at being dishonest. Her mother had looked at her suspiciously more than once.

The lies so far were only the start of it, she knew. She'd have to call Dennis and tell him she couldn't go to the prom. She'd call tonight. It'd be unfair to wait. He'd still have a chance to ask someone else—at least a few days. There'd be a lot of girls who'd go with him even on such short notice.

Somehow she thought of the word *murder*. Murder. She said the word several times, over and over.

They parked near the water. He didn't know what was wrong with her. She had hardly said a word.

"Do you want a cigarette?" he asked, hoping that might start her off.

"No."

He reached over and took her hand. That was another thing he had learned. Whenever she was in one of her moods, just touching her gently seemed to bring her around.

"Stepfather troubles again?"

"No," she answered, not looking at him.

He moved closer to her.

"What's the matter?"

She felt warm against his body, and she tried to forget what she was there to do. She rested her head on his shoulder and wanted to respond in the way he would be expecting her to. More than anything she wished everything could keep going the way it had the last few months. Perhaps she wouldn't tell him. Postpone it. A month. A week. She didn't have to tell him now.

"Relax," he said, smoothing her hair away from her eyes. He lifted her head and put his lips on hers.

But she knew she would have to speak now. It would be stupid to wait. Gently, she moved her lips away and lowered her head to his chest.

He must have moved too soon, he thought. She wasn't ready.

"Are you sure you wouldn't like a cigarette?"

"No, thank you." Her voice was muffled against his shirt.

He lowered himself in the seat. With one hand he continued to stroke her hair.

Somehow he suspected she was up to something different tonight. He never took lightly anything she did. It was usually totally wild or totally calculated, and he could never be positive which it was. She might want something, he thought. She's up to a little bargaining. Like the time he had refused to go to a picnic, and she had held out until she got her way. There was often a method to her madness. He tried to say it jokingly. He thought if he could get her to laugh she'd be all right.

"What do you want this time?"

She lifted her head slowly until she was staring into his eyes. He could tell he had said the wrong thing, but she exploded before he could do anything.

"Get your hands off me! That's what I want!"

He jolted from surprise, hitting his head on the window. Before he recovered, she had flung open the door on her side and started to run down the beach.

"*Liz!*" he called after her. He rubbed the back of his head as he got out of the car.

He watched her run for a moment before he realized she was heading nearer the water.

"Liz!" He started after her.

She ran along the waterline for a distance. The waves were particularly high and breaking close to shore. One wave rushed up the sand and covered her shoes. She almost fell from the wet sand fighting her strides. Finally she slowed to a halt. He was running toward her. She knew that, but she didn't care. All she wanted was him out of her life. Along with her family. Along with everything and everyone.

He caught her before she had gotten far out into the cold water. His legs were numb, and the wind sent a chill through his body as he carried her back to the car. She struck out at him several times. but when he stood her against the car, she was helpless and shaking.

The look of hate in her eyes frightened him.

"Who was that?" Mrs. Holowitz asked.

"Maggie." Dennis sat back down at the dinner table. A moment passed, and he knew his mother and father were studying his face for a clue.

Mrs. Holowitz passed a bowl of whipped potatoes to her son and returned to cutting the steak on her plate. She chewed a small piece of the meat and then broke the silence.

"Is anything wrong?"

"No," Dennis said. He lifted a piece of meat quickly to his own mouth to give him a minute to think. He chewed very slowly, even exaggerating his ruminations to demonstrate that further comment at the moment was impossible. When Mr. Holowitz lifted his head and looked at him, he knew it was an unspoken insistence on an explanation.

"She forgot to copy the history assignment in Miss Blair's class." He looked at them to see if the excuse would appease. "The steak is delicious, Mom," he said, quickly filling his mouth with another large piece.

"Did you do the garbage cans this morning?" Mr. Holowitz asked.

"Yes, he did," Mrs. Holowitz said.

Dennis looked down at his plate. He had just finished saying how good the meat was, so he'd have to finish it. Actually, the sight of it was making him sick. How could Maggie have done it to him? he wondered. He had already rented the tuxedo, paid in advance for it. They said he could pick it up on Friday morning and return it Monday. He had ordered the flowers. The florist had helped him decide on a white orchid because it would go with anything. The purple ones were only five dollars, but the white ones were seven fifty. As he sliced another piece of meat a thread of blood trickled out of the incision. He felt as if the blood were his own.

"I notice you're putting the garbage cans on the grass, and they're killing it," Mr. Holowitz said.

"I'm sorry."

"If you put them closer to the curb, near the cement part, maybe we can save it. I saw some coffee grounds out there too. What happened? A bag break?"

"Yes."

"Got to be careful. More careful, son."

"Yes, Father."

He wouldn't ask anyone else, he knew. It was too close to the prom. He put another piece of meat into his mouth. *Oh, God, what was wrong with him?* He thought everything had been going along fine. He would've asked her to go steady. Maybe that's why she broke the date, he thought. She knew they were getting to that point. Perhaps someone else had asked her. Perhaps she had been using him all these months, just waiting for someone else to come along. Anybody. Anybody was better than Dennis Holowitz. *I'm so ugly,* he thought, grinding the meat between his teeth. *Ugly. I'm sick. I'm ashamed. My clothes are ugly. My face is ugly. My body is ugly. What am I doing alive? I always come back to this point. It's always there. This ugliness. I can't fight it. I'm running out of strength.*

"Out of disinfectant?" Mr. Holowitz asked.

"There's still half a jar under the sink," Mrs. Holowitz preempted, though she knew her husband was addressing their son. "He just forgets to use it."

"I'm sorry," Dennis said. "I'm very sorry."

English Honors 12 H 7   Sean Collins
Mr. Zamborsky   Term Project

A short story: The Circus of Night

Dear Mr. Zamborsky:

    Would you kindly excuse me for
not having completed my short story
assignment. A problem came up at
home, and I'll hand it in as soon as
possible. Thank you. I'm sorry.

                    Sean Collins

12

"MAGGIEEEEEEEEL!"

Maggie heard her name piercing the afternoon air as she left the school building. She was surprised to see Liz waving from near the main gate. Maggie had checked all Liz's morning classes, but Liz had cut them. She had even considered calling Liz's house to see what had happened. But now, there she was, smiling and practically jumping up and down.

"Where have you been?" Maggie's voice scolded.

Liz hugged her and took her arm. They began to walk among the hundreds of bustling students fanning out in all directions.

"He's going to marry me," Liz whispered. She let go of Maggie's arm and skipped a few feet like a child. Maggie caught Liz's hand and forced her to stand still.

"He *is?*"

"He is!" Liz let out a shrill laugh which caused several passing students to stare.

"*Really?*"

"Really."

"Oh, Liz, that's wonderful." Maggie didn't know quite what she was saying, but somehow Liz's happiness was infectious. For a moment another thought crossed her mind. Was it something to be happy about? Of course it was, she decided.

"You *told* him?"

"Naturally I told him." Liz looked at Maggie as

though it were the most absurd question. "But I didn't ask him to marry me. I told him I was pregnant and was going to get an abortion and didn't want to get him involved or to think I was forcing him into anything or pressure him or go to my parents or his or—"

"Slow down," Maggie insisted.

"I told him I wanted two hundred dollars, and I'd take care of the rest. Rod had agreed to set the whole thing up, and he didn't have to worry. He didn't say anything at first." Liz took Maggie's arm again and continued strolling happily along the sidewalk with her. "Then he looked at me and said 'I'll marry you.'"

"Just like that?" Maggie couldn't help laughing, she was so happy. She felt stupid laughing, but she couldn't stop it. It was like hearing the best news in the world.

"When?"

"What do you mean *when?*"

"When are you getting married?"

"After graduation, stupid."

"But . . ."

"I'll be three-and-a-half months. We won't have to tell any of the folks."

"But . . ."

"He thinks he can get some money from his father for school. We'll head for California. He can go to school, and I'll work for a few months. In a couple of years we'll come back, and nobody'll know when we got married."

"What about the baby?"

"We can always say it was premature. Either that or big for its age."

Maggie couldn't resist giving Liz a kiss on the cheek.

"I love him," Liz said. Suddenly she was solemn. "I want to have the baby." Liz stopped walking for a moment and fumbled in her pocketbook. She took out a cigarette and cupped a match against the wind. "Don't you think I'll make a good mother?"

"Yes," said Maggie.

"One hell of a good mother!" Liz exclaimed. Then she burst into laughter.

Sean left school after Mr. Zamborsky's class. He had made arrangements with a friend who worked in the Dean's office to pull out the cut cards for the rest of the day.

He went home and waited alone in his room. Finally the ritual started. The slamming of the front door. The loud bellowing voice. His mother hurrying from some part of the house to meet her husband. Her little cry when he lifted her into the air with a *whoooooop!* The two minute welcome-home-from-the-office routine. Then the silence again except for the opening of the liquor cabinet and the shaking of crushed ice.

Sean gave his father ten minutes to stretch out. He always sat in the same chair, an expensive leather one that lifted his feet up when he leaned back. And by his second drink he'd be in as good a mood as he could be.

"Sean, boy. How are you?" Mr. Collins lifted his glass in a toast.

Sean took a deep breath. He had rehearsed everything, knew just what he'd have to do. He put on a big smile and sat down on a stool near the small bar. It would be a good location: If he felt his face betraying him, he would swivel around and take peanuts from a small candy dish or pretend to need more ice.

"Fine, Dad." He tried for an exuberant smile. "How were things at the office?"

"Get more done at lunch than anywhere else, you know that, boy?"

"*No* kidding?"

"Hell, yes."

A silence fell. He noticed his father nervously stirring his drink. It was now or never and he knew it.

"Dad ..."

"What, son?"

Sean clunked two ice cubes into a glass and filled it

with soda. He swung around with a half-smile on his face.

"A friend of mine's in trouble with a girl and he asked me for advice and I don't know what to tell him."

His father's eyes lit up. "That's what he gets for playing around with the old kazoo." He let out a raucous laugh, and Sean joined him. Mr. Collins stopped in the middle of the laugh, then very seriously he said, "It's not *you*, son, is it?"

Sean smiled. "No."

Mr. Collins starting laughing again.

"If it was you, you'd just tell me right out, wouldn't you, boy? We don't keep secrets between us, do we?"

"No, Dad."

"Course not."

"It's not a good friend, just one of the guys at school. I told him I'd ask you. That's if you don't mind."

"I'll give him advice, don't you worry. Tell him to give me a call."

Sean thought a moment. "No, Dad. He wouldn't do that. He'd feel funny."

"It's *Dennis*, I'll bet!" Mr. Collins howled. "You mean to tell me that skinny toothpick's been—"

"Not Dennis. You don't know this guy. He was in my biology class."

"He sure didn't pay attention." Mr. Collins roared again, then got up from the chair. He mixed himself a drink at the bar. Sean allowed his face to look serious enough for his father to stop joking.

"Well," Mr. Collins started, "I'm sure the routine's the same now as when I had my worries." He moved back to the recliner chair, spilling a few drops of his drink as he got into it. "How pregnant is the girl?"

"About two months."

"Two!" Mr. Collins repeated slowly. "Well, I'd say the first job is for the boy to make sure there really *is* a problem. She might be saying she is to get even with him for something. Does he have money? Money in the family?"

"Some."

"That could be another thing. She might be pulling the whole thing to make sure she catches a husband with a little money."

Sean let that settle for a minute as he sipped his soda. "What if she really *is*?" He turned around to take a handful of peanuts.

Mr. Collins tapped the side of his glass with his fingernail. "Then the guy's got to find out if it's his. She may have been spreading it around, if you know what I mean."

"I don't think—"

"It's the ones you don't think. You just tell that boy to make sure he's the only one, you hear me?"

"Yes, Dad."

"That's what you do."

"Uh-huh."

"Yes, sireee!"

They both sipped their drinks.

Finally Sean spoke. "What if it *is* his?"

"Give me some peanuts, boy."

Sean passed the dish to his father and watched him scoop a big handful into his mouth. He chewed them slowly, thinking—remembering. "Then you get friends."

"Friends?"

"Yep. You get a few friends. You only need a few. Get 'em to call the girl or go up and talk to her. She'll get the point and get scared."

"Dad ..."

"You say the kid's got money. Comes from a money family?"

"Yes. Some."

"Then you tell her to get an operation. You tell that guy to spend a few bucks."

"He said the girl offered . . ." Sean turned back to the bar and added another ice cube to his drink.

"What?"

He turned back and looked at his father. "She offered to get an abortion, but—"

"Then what's the problem?" his father interrupted.

"Is it that simple?"

"Hell, yes! Any one of the doctors in this town'll recommend her for a special Puerto Rican vacation. They do that sort of thing down there like it was pulling a tooth. That's all that little girl needs—a good P.R. weekend."

"Would a doctor in this town arrange that sort of thing, Dad?" Sean asked.

"If the money's right, they'd do a lobotomy. Take my word for it. Even our family doctor. He signs anything I tell him to. That car accident I was in years ago. He knew I didn't have whiplash. Five thousand I got out of that one. Remember?"

"But Dad ..."

"What?"

"Suppose he loves her?"

Mr. Collins coughed and took a sip of his drink. He put his hand to his throat and patted it as if trying to dislodge something. "Loves her?"

"Yes."

"Boy, your friend doesn't know what love is. He can think he loves her now, but if he's thinking of marrying her—forget it! Is he planning on going to college, or is he some kind of dummy?"

"College."

"Well, she'll kill him. She'll kill any chance he ever gets. He'll be a zero. A nobody. You think he'll ever finish college? You wait till he tries to take quantitative chemistry or astrophysics and comes home to a wife and a brat or two. Tell him to cut her out now. There's big things ahead in life. He doesn't know half of them yet. Christ, if it was you, and you were thinking of marrying that little blond you're running around with, I'd slap you right across the face. A regular idiot. Tell your friend to give that girl of his a kick in the behind now and get it over with. A man's got to protect himself. Tell him to ask his father. You do that. His father'll say the same thing. In fact, why the hell didn't he?"

Sean put his glass down on the bar. He started walking slowly away. He knew he'd have to say something, but he was afraid his voice would crack.

"Thank you."

"Why doesn't he ask his own father?"

Sean looked at the angry expression on his father's face, the extended jaw, the powerful eyes—the impatient insistence.

"He can't talk to him," Sean said.

Maggie!!!

I'll bring your dress over tonight. You can tell your Mother I picked it up for you. I bought my own, but you know I appreciated your letting me use yours in case we had to go you know where.

I'm so happy!!! My horoscope said I'm coming into a wonderful time. A beautiful time for all Taurus people. Lots of surprises ahead.

I'm so so so so so happy!!!
Mrs. Sean Collins   Mrs. Sean Collins
Doesn't it look good!
                    Mrs. Sean Collins
Mrs. Sean Collins   What state do
they let you get married in if
you're under 18?
                    love Liz

P.S. I asked for roses for the prom. What is Dennis getting you?
P.P.S. I'm excited! Oh, Maggie, can you imagine what's ahead for me.

13

Maggie had not mentioned it to Liz. Liz had enough problems without knowing about the broken prom date with Dennis. It didn't matter that much. I can use the dress for graduation, Maggie thought. The important thing was she had done everything she could for her friend when she needed her.

That was how she felt about it the night before. It wasn't quite so clear today. Dennis had passed her in the hall after third period. He barely nodded, then kept going. He always stopped and talked any other day, told a joke. Something. They would look for each other at the same spot because it was the only time their paths crossed except for History 158H with Miss Blair.

Something in his eyes had made her feel very strange, sick at heart. It was as if his eyes were saying *"I see you, but I don't want to talk to you. I don't want you to even look at me."* It made her think of the expression "losing face." She had read somewhere that Oriental people drive a knife into their stomach when they lose face. Perhaps it had been in a comic book when she was very young. Somehow she could remember a smiling Oriental lady who had been insulted or disgraced. The smile was one of pride. Dignity. Self-respect. But she had plunged a sword into her side. The caption with the picture had quoted the smiling lady. She was saying something like "Forgive me, but I have lost the honor of my soul."

She had told him it was extremely important, that she felt very bad about having to break the prom date. If anyone wanted to tell him the truth, it would have to be Sean, and there was no indication he had. Otherwise he would certainly have understood. But Sean and Dennis didn't seem to be the close friends they used to be, Maggie had noticed. Maybe something like this he wouldn't tell Dennis. She decided to get a pass from her physics class and look for him down at lunch.

She finally saw him in the crowded cafeteria. He was sitting at a table with some boys she didn't know, but he didn't seem to be talking to them—only concentrating on unwrapping an ice-cream sandwich.

"Hello, Dennis," she said when he looked up.

"Hello." He lowered his head and continued unwrapping the ice cream.

"I thought I'd come down and say *hello*."

He looked up again. "That's nice." He took a bite of the sandwich and glanced at the clock on the rear wall.

She hoped he would help with the conversation. She wondered what she was supposed to do. Come right out with the whole story? Tell him it had been a mistake? That now she wanted to go to the prom? That she had been counting on it as much as him?

"Did they have anything good for lunch?" she asked.

"Hamburgers."

"With old soggy onions?" Maggie laughed, but he didn't join her. He continued eating the ice-cream sandwich, licking around the sides, which had begun to drip.

There was an empty chair right in front of her. She could sit down and force him to talk. He could have been polite enough to ask her. She was going to slide nonchalantly into the seat but couldn't make herself move. The noise in the cafeteria was deafening. She opened her mouth to speak but didn't have the energy. The other boys at the table were beginning to stare at her now, and she knew they wondered why she was standing there. When she looked back at Dennis, it was like looking at a stranger. She turned to look at the wall clock herself. She knew it was just as artificial as his pretending to be absorbed in eating the ice cream. She didn't even read the time—didn't notice the position of the hands of the clock. But the movement. The movement allowed her to create the excuse that she had to leave. Time was making her leave. Time was helping her lie.

"I've got to get back to class."

"Yes," he said.

"So long."

"Yes."

She pushed her way through the lines of students. She wasn't certain why she was crying. She wasn't consciously aware of what had happened or what she felt inside. The only thing she could think of was an Oriental lady with a shining long knife in her hands. A smiling Oriental lady.

Liz saw Sean's car waiting by the main gate. He beeped the horn, and she hurried, almost dropping her books. As soon as she opened the door she saw the roses on the back seat. Beautiful white roses in a transparent plastic box.

"Hi!"

"Hello," he said.

"What are these?" Liz plopped her books down on the floor and reached over the seat to pick up the corsage. "They're beautiful."

"I ordered them from the florist."

"Oh, thank you." She leaned over and kissed him warmly on the mouth. He moved uncomfortably and shifted the car. Then she snapped back to the other end of the seat and lifted the cover. She held the corsage in her hand and smelled one of the small flowers.

"They'll go perfect with my dress."

She switched on the radio and pushed in the cigarette lighter. Sean started to drive away from the school.

"It's white and very low cut. *Fantabulously* sexy." She moved the corsage into different positions and twisted the rearview mirror so she could see herself. The lighter popped out, and she took a cigarette from her pocketbook and lit it.

"Want one?"

"No."

"*There*. White roses. I love them. I can wear my hair down and—owl" She suddenly pulled her hand away from the flowers. "They left the thorns on."

"I'm sorry."

"It's not your fault. They should've cut or waxed them. I can trim them."

"Can you . . ." his voice trailed off.

"What?"

"Can you do that?"

"Sure." She looked at him, puzzled for a moment. "How come you're giving me the flowers now? The prom isn't until tomorrow night."

"I paid for them last week," he said weakly.

"You wanted to make sure they went with my dress? They're perfect! Absolutely perfect. Besides, I can experiment. I want to look just right—for you."

The radio came on too loud, and she turned it down.

"I've got it all figured out," Liz continued. "I spoke to this girl in my gym class who just got here from California, and she said UCLA is the best. So you were right. And we can get an apartment—a decent one without cockroaches—for seventy-five dollars a month. I could earn that myself and still save for the hospital bills . . ."

He tried to concentrate on driving. He didn't know how he would tell her. A half hour before, he had thought it would be best to come right out with it. He had done everything he could. He had the money. Practically everything he had in the bank. He had to tell her. He'd thought about it all night, and there was nothing else to do. His father hadn't been right about everything, but there was truth in some of it. He *hadn't* dated that many girls. By going with Liz, he had cut himself off from a lot of others. There were one or two others at school who were as pretty as Liz. What the hell was he supposed to do? Stop his life?

"Even if we have to tell our folks, I don't care," Liz said, blowing a puff of smoke against the windshield. "I thought about it, and it's of infinitesimal importance. What could they do? Scream for two days? Throw a nicotine fit? After it was over, they'd have to let us get married. Right?"

"I suppose so."

"I mean, it's our lives. We've got to grow up sometime, and they sure haven't been much help."

He wondered if he should just stop the car and get it over. He pressed his hand against his sport jacket to make sure the money was still there. Three hundred dollars. He had never carried three hundred dollars in cash before in his life. It left him with less than a hundred in his savings account. He could say he had to get his transmission fixed. He'd account for it somehow.

"There's a lot of things about me you don't know," Liz said. "I can cook and wash clothes. You never knew I was the domestic type, did you?" She burst into laughter.

"No . . ."

"I can. I make a great roast beef. My mother taught me how to use a meat thermometer. It never goes wrong. We could get a slicing machine, and I'll make you the best lunches to take to school. We can save a lot of money that way."

"I suppose we could . . ."

"Don't you think?"

"Uh-hunh . . ."

Liz pressed one of the buttons on the radio to tune in another station. "Have you thought about a name?"

"What?"

"The baby, stupid. If it's a boy, it'll be *Sean*, of

course. Sean Junior. If it's a girl, I thought we might call her Adriana. Now I know you think that's crazy, and if you hate it, we'll find something else. But I'd like Adriana. I think it's a beautiful name."

Sean pulled the car over to the side of the road. There was a fire hydrant, but he didn't notice it until he had braked to a stop. He had to say it quickly.

"What are we stopping here for?" Liz held the corsage box on her lap.

"Liz . . ."

"What?"

He stared forward. "I thought about it, and I don't think we should."

Liz looked at him. "You don't think we should what?"

"Get married," Sean said in a monotone.

"You don't think . . ." Liz's voice failed her. She took the cigarette out of her mouth and slowly ground it into the ash tray. Then she moved forward in the seat, trying to look at him straight on, as if any moment he would smile, and she'd know he was telling some terrible joke. When he couldn't look at her, she sat back.

They sat there a long while, him staring forward and her looking down at the white roses in the box on her lap. Finally she got the words out.

"What made you change your mind?" She gave him a moment to respond. When he didn't, anger began to replace her numbness. "Was it your father? You told him? Is that what changed your mind?" She pushed her hair back against her head. "Well, it's not going to be that uncomplicated. You can tell him I'm not giving up so easy."

"You said . . ."

"I don't care what I said. What do you think I am? Some kind of whore? And these flowers! What are they supposed to be? A going-away present?"

Sean turned on her. His voice practically roared. He didn't have to hold back any longer. "To hear you talk you'd think I was the only one to blame. You had nothing to do with it!" He remembered the money in his jacket pocket. He reached in and took the bills out. He glanced to make sure it was all there. She looked at his hand as if it were a snake. It came toward her, and when she didn't take the money, he put it on top of the flower box.

She wanted to fling it at him. But now it was a matter of saving herself—not love or hate or anything else. She opened her pocketbook and put the money inside. Her hand reached for the door handle.

"I'm sorry," he said.

As if the touch of the box of flowers was unclean, she set it down on the seat. She picked her books up from the floor of the car. She waited another moment for him to look at her.

"You son of a bitch," she said.

She slammed the door, and he was alone.

Dear Maggie —

Please meet me during 5th period in te girls room on the 3rd floor. Cut your history class. I _have to_ talk to you.

Liz

14

MAGGIE LOOKED DOWN at the dress she was wearing. It was the nicest she'd ever owned.

"I don't understand why you've got to leave already. Can't you wait until your father gets home?" Mrs. Tobin asked. "He'd be so proud of his beautiful daughter. Absolutely beautiful, really, Maggie."

"Liz has to help me make up, Mother."

"You girls wear too much makeup as it is." Mrs. Tobin helped Maggie with a light shawl so it draped evenly around her shoulders. "I wish I was your age again, Maggie. I really do."

Maggie moved to the hall mirror and rearranged the shawl.

"Life was so carefree. I hope you appreciate it."

"Yes, Mother."

"You've got plenty of time to grow up, so have a good time now."

"I will, Mother."

Maggie checked her purse, trying to hide her nervousness as her mother continued to stare.

"Do you think the shawl will be warm enough?" Mrs. Tobin asked.

"Yes."

"Absolutely beautiful," her mother repeated.

"Thank you."

Maggie kissed her mother, then quickly opened the front door and started down the walk.

"I never forgot my senior prom, Maggie," Mrs. Tobin called after her. "Never."

Maggie gave a final wave when she reached the sidewalk, then hurried down the street. By the time she had reached the corner of Howard Avenue, the car was waiting. She got in the front seat without saying a word. She couldn't even look at him.

"What took you so long?" Rod's voice was nasty.

"I'm on time."

"Like hell you are."

Liz leaned toward the dresser mirror, trying to finish putting on her lipstick. She was late and didn't want the car horn blaring outside. *Avoid complications. Explanations. Just smile and get out of the house.* Her elbow accidentally hit something on the edge of the dresser. It fell to the floor with a crash.

"Liz!" Her mother's voice came from downstairs.

"It was an accident!" Liz yelled.

"What was it?"

"The Madonna!"

"Oh, Liz!" her mother cried.

In her nervousness she began to paint too far over her lip line. Then she found herself running around the room doing a lot of little silly things. She tried the black shoes on three times. Finally she settled for the white ones, to match the dress. She tried on a pair of earrings but her hands were shaking so badly she couldn't adjust them properly. She teased and sprayed her hair a dozen times. Anything to delay.

Her foot hit a piece of the broken statue, and she kicked it into a corner. She couldn't help remembering the words: *Pray to the Madonna that you be forgiven. Your sins of lust must be forgiven. Your sins of omission. Pray to the Madonna for one day you could murder. Pray to the Madonna.*

"Are you almost ready?" Mrs. Palladino's voice broke in on Liz's thoughts.

Liz checked to make certain she had the money.

"Liz!"

"I'm coming!"

She took a last look in the dresser mirror. She wouldn't cry, she told herself. Steel, she would be as cold and impersonal as steel.

Mrs. Palladino was beaming at the bottom of the stairs.

"Look at our girl. Look at our little girl!"

Mr. Palladino emerged from the living-room archway. He was trying his best to smile. Liz took one look at him and felt the moment had all happened once before.

"Isn't it a lovely dress!" Mrs. Palladino exclaimed, pushing her husband forward, as though prodding a child to recite a poem.

"You look very pretty tonight," Mr. Palladino said.

Liz stared at him. Her hands hung helplessly at her sides. She wanted to turn around and run back to her room—run up the stairs and slam the door behind her. At the same time she wanted to tell them, tell them everything.

A car horn beeped outside. Her father opened the front door. Her mother said something. She didn't hear it. They were waving from the doorway as she got into the back seat of the car. A funeral. She could only think of a funeral. She watched them from the car window as it began to move. Then they disappeared.

"The cigarette lighter back there doesn't work," Rod said. He pushed in the one on the dashboard, but Liz had already lit a match. She inhaled deeply. Then she looked at Maggie for the first time.

"You all right?" Maggie asked.

Liz nodded.

"Got what I want?" Rod asked.

Liz opened her purse and counted out some money. She handed it forward.

"Ten more for gas and tolls."

"Can you put the heater on?" Liz asked.

"No."

"Why not?"

"I don't feel like it."

Maggie reached out and touched Liz's hand. For a long time they rode in silence. When the car reached a toll booth at Goethals Bridge, Maggie decided Liz wanted to be left to her own thoughts. She turned around and looked at the river below. The factories along the shore grew smaller as the car climbed higher on the bridge roadway. It was like being in an airplane she thought. When she looked at her watch, she knew it was about the time all the others would be arriving at the prom.

"What is he like?" Liz asked.

Rod looked at her in the rearview mirror. "Who?"

"The doctor."

Maggie turned around again. "I'm going in with you, Liz."

"You're waiting in the car with me. She goes in alone. Are you listening?" Rod turned away from the wheel to look at them.

"I hear you," Liz said.

"His wife is the nurse. She'll tell you how to fill out the papers. What to write. Like you're there about a cold. She'll make you lie about your age and give a phony address. You do it just the way she says. And you sign the papers. If you open your smart-ass mouth, they'll kick you out so fast you won't know what hit you."

About an hour later the car pulled off the main highway. They traveled along a service road for a few miles, then came to a town and drove down a street lined with large old homes. The car stopped in front of a house with porch lights burning brightly. It was nothing like Maggie had imagined. The front lawn was meticulously trimmed. The exterior of the house seemed clean and white. A small lighted sign hung near the sidewalk. It said "*J. La Salle, M.D.*"

"Can't I go in with her?" Maggie asked.

"I said *No*." Rod pushed Maggie's seat forward. "We're late, you know."

Liz sat frozen. She watched him lean across and open the door.

"Hurry up," he said.

Liz got out slowly. She stood on the sidewalk a moment, then started toward the house. Maggie watched her silhouette against the porch lights as she went up the steps. She rang the bell and a moment later disappeared inside.

"If she's not out in half an hour, I'm calling the police," Maggie said, her voice cracking.

"You move out of this car, and all you're getting is a fist in the face."

Maggie started to cry.

"I told her to leave you out of this," he said.

"I'll bet you did."

"You're a real retard, you are, honey. They don't hardly make 'em like you anymore."

Maggie turned her face away and concentrated on one of the porch lights. The rays burned her eyes, and she stared until she had to blink. She read the name on the sign over and over. "J. La Salle, M.D., J. La Salle, M.D., J. La Salle, M.D." She wouldn't forget the name. If anything happened to Liz, she'd see they found him. They'd get him.

It seemed an hour had gone by before Maggie saw the figure on the porch. She wasn't certain at first, but the way it moved, the little skip-walk, it had to be Liz. Maggie couldn't believe she wasn't moving slowly after what she must have been through. In a second the door was open and Liz bounced into the back seat.

"Hi!" Liz laughed.

"Everything OK?" Rod asked.

"Yep," Liz said.

Maggie couldn't believe it. "It's all over?"

Liz pulled out a stick of gum, unwrapped it, and stuck it in her mouth. "Uh-huh," she said. She lit a cigarette and sat back as if she didn't have a care in the world.

"Drugs?" Rod asked, starting the car. "That's what he gave my old girl friend."

"Uh-huh," Liz mumbled.

"What kind of drugs?" Maggie asked.

"I don't want to talk about it," Liz said. "Put the radio on."

As the car pulled away Liz bolted forward and kissed Maggie on the cheek.

"It's all over," she said. "It's all over, Maggie."

Liz insisted on stopping for something to eat at a roadside stand. Maggie refused to get out of the car, but at the same time she didn't want Liz to go alone. There was something shrill and hysterical about Liz's voice, and it worried Maggie.

"You'll look silly."

"What do I care?" Liz said, getting out of the car and heading toward the stand. "If they never saw a girl wear a formal dress to a hot-dog stand, they're going to see one now."

Rod sat silent next to Maggie for a minute. Then he said, "I'll be right back." He took the car keys with him as he went.

Finally Liz returned. "I got you two hot dogs," Liz said, pushing them through the window at Maggie.

"I'm not hungry."

"No?"

"How can you eat?" Maggie asked.

"I'm starved!" Liz exclaimed. She squeezed into the back seat and continued to talk as she munched on the food. "Where's Rod?"

"I think he went to the men's room."

Liz checked the ignition switch immediately. "Took the keys with him?"

"Yes."

"Do you think he doesn't trust us?" Liz laughed.

"You feel all right?" Maggie asked.

"Fine."

Rod came back and got in the car. He slammed the door.

"I'll get off at Liz's house," Maggie told him.

"Did you get me anything?" Rod asked.

"You can have three of them," Liz said, practically shoving the hot dogs toward him.

He put them on the center armrest and started the car. In a few minutes they were back on the highway.

Maggie watched Rod eat as he drove. He was practically pushing the hot dogs down his throat. It was like watching an animal eat, she thought. Not tasting the food, just cramming it down to fill up its stomach, one bite after the other. The mustard lined his lips. At one point a strand of sauerkraut was smeared against his chin. Then, after he had finished, she watched him wipe his face, one hand on the wheel, the other moving over every inch of his face. When that had been completed, he worked on his hair. She watched him look into the rearview mirror a dozen times to check it. Finally, the facade rebuilt, he began to smile. Now that his appetite had been appeased, she thought, now he could smile.

"Here we are," Rod announced as the car came to a halt. "I'll see you, but don't you see me." He laughed.

Maggie turned around in her seat to help Liz. At first she thought Liz was only sleeping.

"Liz?"

Liz didn't answer. There was something about her position that seemed unnatural.

"Liz?" Maggie said louder.

She was leaning forward, her head down. Her hands were pressed against her stomach. Maggie could see she was crying as she reached out for her shoulders. She tried to lift her slowly, but Liz stopped her.

"Liz, what should I do?" Maggie asked. She looked at Rod, but she could see he was just as frightened as she was.

"What is it?" Maggie screamed.

"I'm bleeding," Liz managed to say. "Oh, God, I'm bleeding."

Maggie was momentarily paralyzed with fear. Then suddenly it was as if she could see only one way out of the nightmare. She opened the car door and started to run toward the house.

"Don't tell them. Don't let them know," Liz spit out, raising her head in spite of the pain.

Maggie ran toward the front door. She saw a light on in an upstairs bedroom. Again and again she rang the bell. Someone had to be home.

"Let me die!" Liz screamed from the car. "Let me die, you lousy traitor!"

English Honors 12 Hx   Sean Collins
Mr. Zamborsky

Short story assignment (make-up)

THE CIRCUS OF BLACKNESS

The hordes of people filled the seats long before the grand march was to begin. They had come early to make sure they had a good seat for the bizarre pageant about to unfold before them.

They were a strange audience. A woman dressed in silver waved a dark flag from a ringside seat. Her eyes were burning like a phantom's as she screamed for the show to begin. A stout man stomped on the wooden planks of the bleachers, the sweat pouring off him into pools at his feet. A skinny woman in the last row let out a witch's laugh and threw blue tinsel in the air.

The ringmaster entered, a small spotlight clinging to his ghostly face. The crowd burst into applause for they knew the festivities were about to start. He lifted a whistle to his lips, blew it loud and clear, and the whole tent became ablaze with floodlights. The band began to play a weird and haunting melody. Black curtains at the far end of the arena parted.

First came the monstrous elephants
painted in colors of an evil rainbow.
Their trumpeting reverberated in the air,
and for a moment the crowd held its
breath. Behind them came the caravan of
wild cats, lions with their proud manes
tossing, the spotted panthers with glaring
yellow eyes. The animals looked as hungry
as the ugly audience that cheered them
madly as they roared their jungle cries.

The crowd laughed when the clown walked
by. The most spectacular, colossal clown
in the circus of blackness. It was an old
man staggering around the arena. In his
hands he carried a huge idol made of
toothpicks. Billions of tiny splinters had
been glued together to make the magnificent
idol. Following him was a fat acrobat with
a loud voice that boomed in gratitude for
the ovation of the crowd. Holding on to
the end of his red cape were two squat
puppets dressed like Buddhas, fat tiny
Buddhas waddling after the acrobat.

What strange thing was going to happen?
What was the crowd really waiting for? It
had to be more than the parade of gro-
tesquerie that marched proudly by!

A hush fell as some new figures entered
from behind the dark curtains. The band
had even stopped for a moment. Then it
started a new theme, a theme so beautiful
only the new arrivals seemed to move with
it. It was as if the entire circus had
frozen to watch the star attraction take
its place in the center of the ring.

Six pygmies commenced their promenade
toward the middle of the tent. Like slaves
they towed behind them a huge ghastly cart
covered with white silk. It was impossible
to see what was hidden beneath the silk,
but there seemed to be two large wooden
masts of some sort, projections giving the
whole cart the appearance of a galleon. A
magical, enchanted seacraft being towed by

the six demonic pygmies. Standing at the
front of the cart were a young boy and
girl. They seemed to be hypnotized—as if
they were in a world completely apart
from the ugliness which surrounded them.
Together they held a small wooden box in
their hands.

The boy and girl remained on the cart as
the ringmaster approached. The crowd became suddenly delirious with joy because
the finale was about to begin. With a
ruthless snap of his whip the ringmaster
tore the silk cover from the cart, and a
strange machine was revealed. Only then
did the boy and girl make their single
plea. Slowly they raised the wooden box
upward toward the heavens, but the crowd
roared. There would be no mercy.

The ringmaster took the box from them,
and out of it he lifted a tiny baby. He
walked to the edge of the cart and extended the infant to the boy. The boy felt
the arms of the acrobat reach around him,
forcing him to hold the baby. A witch ap-
peared and made the girl do her part to
prepare the proper place. When everything
was ready, the boy was forced to put the
baby's neck in the slot between the two
huge poles that reached up toward the top
of the tent. Once he resisted, but the
fat, evil acrobat was too strong for him.
The girl would no longer look, no matter
how the witch twisted her face upward to
see the shiny piece of metal at the top of
the poles. The Circus of Blackness was
coming to its climax, the crowd roared for
the ultimate act. The band began to play.
The ringmaster blew his whistle, and the
dwarf cut the rope that held back the
blade. Its dazzling razor edge fell downward toward the baby's neck as screams of
joy from the audience deafened the cries
of the boy and girl.

A=

You have a remarkable imagination.. Very cryptic!

Mr. Zambrosky

June 20
Tuesday

Dear Liz:

I have called your house every day for the last week. Your mother says she never wants me to call again. She says _you_ don't want me to call either. Liz, I only did what I thought was best for you. I was so scared. I thought you were dying. I thank God you didn't, Liz. I asked about you in Mr. Zamborsky's office, and he said you can still graduate. A general diploma is better than nothing. You can make up credits later and get an academic one.

If you don't answer this, then I will know you really don't want me as a friend any more. But even so, I've got to tell you that I am very grateful for all the wonderful times we had together — you and me and Dennis and Sean. You are the only one out of the whole crazy world that tried to give me confidence in myself, and I'll never forget you for that. Never, Liz. Please answer me Liz,

Please!
Sincerely,
Maggie Tobin

*It is with great pleasure that
the Senior Class of Franklin High School
requests the honor of your presence
at its graduation exercises
to be held on Thursday, June twenty-seventh,
at eight-thirty p.m. in the
main auditorium*

15

KEEP YOUR VOICES DOWN," Mr. Zamborsky shouted. "They'll hear you in the auditorium!" He blew his whistle several times and darted between the lines of boys and girls.

"Students! Make sure you're in the same place assigned at rehearsal. Boys on the left side of the hall. Girls on the right. Hurry." *Wwwwwrrrrrrrrrrrrrl!*

Suddenly a silence spead down the corridor. The band had started to play. At rehearsals, everyone had howled at the screeching clarinets. They had hooted the homely little girl who played the cymbals and laughed at the spectacled boy who pounded the big bass drum. They had jeered and dismissed every part of the ceremony. But now, trancelike, almost terrified, they took their places in line. Mr. Zamborsky gave a signal. The marshals opened the rear doors of the auditorium, and the music leaped out with deafening volume. The slow sounding of the drum pervaded everywhere like the heartbeat of a giant, and the lines began to move, slowly, solemnly. Miss Blair stood at the entrance, making certain each student was in step. Hundreds of parents and relatives stood facing the rear of the auditorium as the first boy and girl stepped into view.

"Good luck, ladies and gentlemen," Miss Blair whispered as the graduates passed by. Several of the girls began to cry. The boys pulled back their shoulders and set their jaws. They hadn't rehearsed that. It was automatic, a reflex. For some, this was the first time they had felt the power of ritual.

At first, Maggie couldn't find the beat. Finally, near the entrance, she fell in step. "An arm's length between me and the girl in front of me," she kept repeating to herself. As she moved farther into the auditorium she saw her mother and father smiling from their seats near the middle aisle. There was such pride in their smiles it was all she could do to keep from bursting into tears. She gave a smile in return and pretended not to notice the tears running down her mother's face. Flashbulbs were going off, and Maggie had to close her eyes from moment to moment to erase their blinding stains. The entrance seemed to be lasting forever. Then finally she turned into an empty row and was thankful when she reached her seat. She had to stand in front of it until the rest of the graduates had entered. During the singing of the national anthem she couldn't help but look back again at her mother. After a short prayer the audience was given the signal to sit down.

Maggie sat perfectly still. She kept her hands on her lap and tried to concentrate on all the speeches. It seemed to be making polite sense, but so much of it sounded hollow, shallow. She tried to understand exactly why, and the only word she could think of was *disappointment*. Perhaps that was it.

This should be such a big day, she thought. Everyone talks about it, writes about it. I don't feel so joyous. She could see Dennis now across the auditorium in the same row as she was. She was on the right side, and he was on the far left—across the center aisle. There were dozens of other profiles between them, each one protruding a fraction of an inch farther than the one before it. It reminded her of looking into a set of double mirrors at a carnival. When she leaned forward, she was able to see Sean on the far side, three rows behind. He was so tall, and Mr.

Zamborsky had made everyone line up according to size places.

For a moment the principal's voice intruded on her thoughts. " ... and last but not least, tonight represents a triumph for your parents who have loved you, encouraged you, and prayed for you to reach this exciting and marvelous time in your lives ..."

Maggie decided to think about Pierre Jefferson. At least that was a little exciting. He had invited her to a party after graduation, and the more she thought about it, the more she wondered if she had done the right thing. He was so square and intellectual, but she had always admired him. He was much better-looking than Dennis, and it sort of scared her. *Just my old complexes*, she decided. *I'm really worried about my shape or how clumsy I'll be or some other nonsense.* She remembered thinking all those things when he had called on the phone. Somehow she had managed to say Yes.

"You *will?*" Pierre had sounded surprised.

"Yes," Maggie had said more firmly.

Maggie leaned forward to get another look at Dennis. *How sad he looks*, she thought. He wasn't looking her way. He just seemed to be looking at the floor.

She sat back in her seat again. *Oh, is there any point to anything?* she wondered. *I'm the one that's downcast and defeated. I'm the one that has ended up alone. I'm frightened. Half the kids around me will be married in a few years or so. They'll have kids of their own, and I'll meet them pushing baby carriages in the supermarket.*

"Oh, Maggie Tobin! Aren't you married yet?"

"No, I'm not," she'd have to say.

I'm going down, not up, she thought. *Down.*

"The history award goes to Pierre Jefferson ..."

A round of polite applause broke out in the auditorium. Maggie snapped out of her thoughts for a moment and watched Pierre stride across the stage. He did look very handsome in his tuxedo, she thought.

When that was over, she lowered her gaze to where

her hands lay almost waxlike on her lap. For a second she felt as though she were looking at the hands of a stranger. They didn't seem to be a part of her. She looked at her fingers: the few creases near each knuckle the uneven shapes at the base of the nails. It was the first time she had actually looked at her own hands with the same scrutiny she gave to other people's. The fingers on the white dress, the fingers which might never have an engagement ring on them. The shoes, the white shoes. She looked down and saw a scuff on the white leather. I'm still so gross, she thought. The shoes, the white dress, the corsage. It was all like a wedding day. Her own wedding. The only thing missing was the ring.

"Something old, something new; something borrowed, something blue." She laughed at her own thoughts. There was something absolutely ludicrous about sitting there pretending it was her wedding day. "Something old, something new; something borrowed ..." She couldn't stop the saying from running through her mind. Blue, she thought. I feel blue. That must be the blue part they talk about. Something old. What's something old? The whole graduation exercise! They were old. The entire ceremony going on in this auditorium is older than the hills. Older than anything she could think of—the Babylonians, the Egyptians. They must have had graduation exercises of some sort, some kind of ritual.

"Something borrowed." She couldn't think of something borrowed at first. Then she remembered a voice saying " ... and last but not least, tonight represents a triumph for your parents who have loved you, encouraged you, and prayed for you to reach this exciting and marvelous time ..." The speeches! They were filled with borrowed things—borrowed over and over again until the words were nothing more than a series of clichés. Tedious worn mouthings. *No wonder none of us is paying attention. They're not new words for us. They're the old ones. The ones borrowed from another time.*

"Something new." That was all she needed now, and the saying would be complete. "Something old, something new; something borrowed, something blue." She was blue, the exercises were old, the speeches were borrowed. What was new?

She was aware that tears had started to run down her face. Was it shame? Was that what was new? She had promised herself she wouldn't think about Liz any more, but now she couldn't help it. Maybe it was shame that was new to all of them. Different kinds of shame, different degrees. She turned to look at Sean again as though his face would hold some clue. She could still hear Liz's voice confiding in her.

"Oh, Maggie, you don't know him like I do," Liz had once said. "He seems a little conceited but he isn't."

Liz used to tell me almost everything, she remembered. Sean had so many problems, Liz always said. Maggie felt like yelling across the auditorium at him, she was so angry. *"Are you satisfied?"* That's what she'd like to ask him. *"Are you satisfied about what you did to Liz? When you give someone the kind of shame you gave her—the kind that stops her from showing her face in public—that's something to blow your head off about, Sean Collins!"*

The choir members filed past Maggie. She took out a handkerchief and wiped her eyes. Moments later Mrs. Voight, the music teacher, raised her hand to start the singing.

Mine eyes have seen the glory of the coming
   of the Lord,
He hath trampled out the vintage where the
   grapes of wrath are stored. . . .

Perhaps nothing is new, Maggie thought, nothing is new in the whole world. Nothing her mother or father or the principal or Miss Blair or Mr. Zamborsky or

Miss Fanuzzi—nothing anyone said was new. She remembered Miss Fanuzzi's advice about how to stop a boy if he was getting too passionate. She could still hear herself suggesting going to get a hamburger. Dennis had just kissed her once, and she was screaming for a hamburger.

Maggie slouched down in her seat and listened to the choir. She just never had felt so out of place before in her life. I'm in a strange room, she thought. I don't belong here. I want to get myself out of this auditorium, lift myself away and above everybody. She looked at the right side of the stage, where a faded old curtain was hanging. Her eyes followed the proscenium arch up to the loudspeaker on the wall, then moved along the archway high above the stage. At first she stared only at a painted ceiling. Then suddenly she was surprised to see a cherubic face smiling down at her. The form of an angel with large, spread wings became apparent in the plaster ceiling. It had obviously been painted over many times, but it was still visible if you looked hard enough. The hundreds of times she'd sat in the auditorium, she'd never noticed it before—an angel blowing a trumpet.

But that was the story of her life, she decided, always looking and only seeing part of what was there. Inside, though, she knew she had come a long way since she had worn cockeyed eyebrows and pleated dresses. She had to laugh at the thought of her and Liz sitting in the auditorium all those months ago. She remembered the time she had asked who the weird-looking boy was sitting next to Sean—the boy with the baggy green sweater. For a moment the memory seemed so real she wanted to turn and find Liz next to her again. Turn the clock back and start all over again.

Maggie felt suddenly sick inside. She put her head in her hands, and the girl sitting next to her tapped her gently.

"Are you all right?" the girl asked.

"Yes," Maggie whispered. "Thank you."

Maggie turned to see if her mother had noticed anything wrong. She was still sitting with her father, smiling in the sea of faces. Maggie looked back up at the cherub's face, and at that moment it seemed as if all life was nothing but seeing more of the things that were always right in front of your nose. Everything in her life that had ever upset her seemed silly when she looked back at it. She felt a slight chill run through her when she realized she was always looking back at a silly, foolish girl. She wondered if in a short time she'd remember how miserable she was on this graduation night and whether it would all seem as naive and idiotic. Was that what life was going to be? Just going from one year to the next feeling slightly less ridiculous? Was that what all the talk about *maturing* was? *Mature* this and *mature* that!

Before she knew what had happened, the graduates were standing. She was a split second late, and her row of girls had begun to move toward the stage. Mr. Zamborsky was calling out the names and handing the diplomas to the principal. At a signal from Miss Blair, a boy or girl would move across the stage, shake the principal's hand, and receive a small scroll tied with a thin blue ribbon. When Maggie's name was called, she started toward the center of the stage. A moment before, the fear she would trip had crossed her mind, but as she approached the principal she knew that wasn't going to happen. With one glance she had seen the million things Liz had somehow taught her: the microphone wire protruding slightly into her path, the music stand carelessly left near the far side, the proper place to pause in order not to block the principal and yet be seen by the audience.

She returned to her seat and sat down. Once more she looked up to be sure the angel was really there—and it was. At the same time she couldn't help wondering how many other secrets were surrounding her. Would she have to wait until some time in the future in order to know why she felt so terrible?

She watched Sean accept his diploma, and somehow she suddenly felt very sorry for him. He'd have his punishment, she thought. For the rest of his life he'd remember Liz. He could go on to college and date dozens of other girls. He could get married and have children—but from time to time he'd remember. Just before going to sleep, perhaps, in a dream. He'd have to remember Liz and something he couldn't be very proud of. The past wasn't that easy to get away from.

Maggie turned and saw her mother's eyes still fixed on her. It was always there in one form or another, the past—always lurking, smiling, no matter how you painted over it. You could yell at it and insist it didn't exist. You could fight it and say it was gone. But it was still inside of you all along, Maggie knew.

There was a crash of cymbals, and Maggie was jolted back into the reality of the graduation. Everyone was on his feet. The recessional had begun. She moved sideways along the row. It had been easier filing in because all the seats were up, but now many of them were down. Dennis was edging toward the center aisle at the same time as she. Their eyes met, but he looked away. He had reached the center aisle a moment before her and started for the rear of the auditorium. She was in a different line and a few feet behind, and as she looked at the back of his head she was overwhelmed by the fact that at that very moment she was creating her own past. To let Dennis go his way and for her to go her own without even saying a word would be a memory she'd have to have for the rest of her life. It seemed as if it was something Liz should have known, and Sean. They should have known what they were risking. The present becomes the past, and it continues inside you.

The hallway and lobby outside the auditorium were mobbed. Some of the girls were crying. A few of the boys looked stunned. Most were talking and laughing loudly, relieved that the tension was over. The first parents to pour out of the auditorium squealed with joy.

"Congratulations, Maggie!" Helen Bordanowitz said explosively.

"Same to you," Maggie said, continuing through the crowd.

At last she saw him at the end of the lobby. He was leaning against the wall next to a bulletin board covered with photographs of foreign countries. She knew he saw her coming, and she wasn't surprised to see him turn away. It didn't matter though, because she knew what she had to do.

"Hello, Dennis," she said.

He looked surprised she had spoken. He answered softly, "Hello, Maggie."

"I wanted to congratulate you," she said, smiling warmly, "and tell you how handsome you look in your tuxedo."

"Thank you," he said stiffly. Then he quickly added, with a grin, "It's rented."

They both laughed nervously.

She hesitated a moment, trying to find the right words. "I wanted to call you . . ."

"I wanted to call you too."

"You did?"

They laughed at their sudden seriousness.

"I guess you know what happened by now," Maggie said.

"Yes," he said.

Maggie glanced downward a moment and noticed her fingers were kneading her pocketbook. She looked up again. "Well, I just wanted you to know I wish you the greatest success in life." She extended her hand to him, and he took it. Then she smiled.

"We'll keep in touch," Dennis said. He raised his hand to check his bowtie.

"Yes," she said.

"Maybe we'll go to a movie sometime."

"That would be nice," she said. "Or at least go for a hamburger."

They both laughed.

"Remember *Primitive Love* and the Wambesi?" Dennis asked.

They laughed again.

"Good-bye, Dennis," she said.

He looked at her but didn't speak.

She kissed him quickly on the cheek. "I'll always remember you," she said, and she started down the hall.